© 2020 Aidan Hughes and The Estate of Malcolm Bennett.
Published by Eyewear Publishing. All rights reserved.
ISBN 978-1-912477-72-2

Created, written & illustrated by Malcolm Bennett and Aidan Hughes.
Resurrected and fly-fucked by Nigel Proktor.
Words of praise by Vince Raison.

*No part of this publication may be reproduced, stored in a retrieval system or transmitted, in any form by any means, electronic, mechanical, photocopying, recording or otherwise without the written consent of the publishers. Heretofore, thereafter and in accordance with the boring laws of England.* **OFFICIAL!**

**WARNING!** Do not attempt to drive, operate machinery or approach rutting livestock while under the influence of this book.

Reading this book aloud in a public place may result in serious injury. **YOURS!**

Printed and bound by TJ International Ltd, Padstow, Cornwall.

# BRUTE!

## THE COMPLETE PULP NASTIES
## 1984 – 1989

Created, written & illustrated by
Malcolm Bennett
& Aidan Hughes

Wallasey – Prague – Valhalla

**FOR MALCOLM,
MY COMRADE & BROTHER**

# Contents

Malcolm Bennett & Aidan Hughes would like to express their deep regard for those authors who gave their lives during the Falklands Conflict (1982-82) : R.I.P. Rod Corkhill, Lawford Gates, I. Barker, Jack Liverpool, Keith Eastwood & Kurt 'Kid' Caldwell.

| | |
|---|---|
| 15 | PUB ACTION! by Lawford Gates |
| 17 | THE LAZY BARMAN by Semon Dye |
| 18 | BROOKWOOD by Rod Corkhill |
| 21 | THE CALL by Jack Liverpool |
| 22 | BLOKE-U-POKE! by Jock Hudson |
| 23 | JIM! by Jack Liverpool |
| 24 | BRUTE FORCE! by Lawford Gates |
| 28 | SHOOT! By Moaner Lisa |
| 30 | FRANK! By Chris Von Cushing |
| 32 | WHEN MORNING WAS OVER by Dick Skinhead |
| 34 | THE THING! by Barry Kraftwerk |
| 35 | THE PIG FARMER AND THE BOY by Jack Armstrong |
| 36 | HOLE AHOY! By C. Mann |
| 39 | JIM MALLET STRIKES BACK! by Lawford Gates |
| 40 | PUG! by Pubwash Kershaw |
| 42 | JOB'S NEW OVERALLS by Kurt 'Kid' Caldwell |
| 43 | THE GRINDER AND THE WHIRLWIND by Q. Ball & Bork End |
| 44 | VIC! by Lawford Gates |
| 46 | DAY OF THE PIG by Kurt 'Kid' Caldwell |
| 53 | TWIX! by Pat Women |
| 54 | THE PARABLE OF THE YOUNG MEN AND THE JOB by Pierre le Poisson |
| 56 | THE DIARY OF A DEVELOPING WEREWOLF by I. Barker |
| 57 | GREASEBY by Gut Fullercourage |
| 59 | THE WILD WEST by Hank Hudson |
| 60 | THE VIKINGS! by Knüt Sküt |
| 62 | THE EARTH AND THE SOIL by Keith Eastwood |
| 64 | PICK-UP! by Dicken Cider |
| 67 | SCAB! By Arthur 'King' Hoffa |
| 68 | BLIZZARD! by Wolf Winter |
| 69 | THE PIG FARMER AND THE BOY 2 by Jack Armstrong |

70   P.A.C. MEN! by Gut Fullercourage
74   THE FIGHT! by Buster Speedbag
76   THE ELECTION by Kurt 'Kid' Caldwell
79   THE ANGLER! by Rod Nodoffalott
80   THE JOB! by Lump Hammer
82   MUGVILLE by Hank Hudson
83   THE REBEL by Pierre le Poisson
85   WORMWOOD by Rod Corkhill
88   JOCK! by Fin Gerderhard
89   BETWEEN TWO LUNGS by Lump Hammer
93   NEVER SAY DIE! by Stunt Dubble
94   THE GAMBLER! by Krap Kerouac
97   ME, SEAMAN by C. Lyons
99   THE SUBBUTEO KING by Bill Bott
100  TWAT! by Gut Fullercourage
105  NO ONE GETS BETWEEN A WOMAN AND HER ICE CREAM
       by Snr. Gael Barcia Rath Martinez-Velazquez Snr.
106  QUACK! by Carlsberg Norsebarr
108  CRAZY HOT DAY by Keith Eastwood
113  WOLF! by Keith Eastwood
114  THE PLOT! by Lump Hammer
115  PUB HAWK! by Flt. Lt. Douglas Lager D.S.O. in Bar
118  THE WOLFS by Jack Bastard
119  THE LEGEND OF PAUL DIAMOND by Keith Eastwood
122  A BROKEN MAN by Keith Eastwood
124  DAGGER! by Lawford Gates
127  WHEN I WAS YOUNG by Vic Wipeout
128  A TOWN CALLED EARLY by Keith Eastwood
132  THINGY! by Edgar Rice-Krispy
137  THE MATCH! by Bell End
138  JUNGLE BOY by William Rice-Krispy
139  NORTON BIKEMAN by Isla Mann
150  OFF-DUTY by Chad Crisis
151  GRAILWOOD by Anon (document found at 180, Rennes le Chateau, France)
152  ¡TOROS! by Ernie Hemmings

| | |
|---|---|
| 155 | **THE GLADIATORS!** by Homer Sexual |
| 157 | **PARA!** by D. Day Landing |
| 158 | **THE SEA!** by Jack Liverpool |
| 159 | **DING!** by Arthur Terryweight |
| 162 | **WHEN WOMEN COME TO PUBS** by Scally Onassis |
| 164 | **ME, MANIAC!** by Rick D. Spleen |
| 166 | **CUB-COP** by I. Barker |
| 167 | **DYKE!** by Les B. Ian |
| 169 | **I, THE BREWERY** by Lawford Gates |
| 171 | **OUTBACK** by Bill Abongtree |
| 172 | **THE WEDDING** by Kurt 'Kid' Caldwell |
| 173 | **DR. O!** by Ian Phelgm |
| 176 | **SHERWOOD** by Rod Corkhill |
| 179 | **FAG!** by Dean P. de Phial & Jim Teacher |
| 180 | **NUTTER!** By Bratt Paki |
| 183 | **SUMO!** By Mrs. Sony Sanyo |
| 184 | **TOP!** by Bradford Grimsby-Scunthorpe |
| 186 | **HOOLIGAN!** by Richard Alan |
| 187 | **CUB-COP 2** by I. Barker |
| 188 | **THE HOLY ALE** by Pierre le Poisson |
| 190 | **STINGY'S** by Karl Lagerfield |
| 191 | **PA!** by Kurt 'Kid' Caldwell |
| 193 | **SPOCK OFF!** by Capt. Slog |
| 194 | **THE HORROR!** by Chris Von Cushing |
| 197 | **SOHO!** By Henri le Frogoeuf |
| 198 | **BLOODBATH!** by C. Mann |
| 200 | **THE HANGING TREE** by Kurt 'Kid' Caldwell |
| 204 | **POLICE BUSINESS!** by Ford Stockwood |
| 206 | **BINGO!** by Tony Hitchbloch |
| 210 | **THE WOLF!** by Jack Bastard |
| 211 | **9½ SECS!** by Germaine Gridlips |
| 214 | **ADMAN** by T. Leaf |
| 216 | **COP!** by SPG Thug |
| 217 | **CONTENDER** by Wallasey Checkpoint |
| 218 | **EPIC!** by H.G. Verne |
| 220 | **THE MIRACLE** by Keith Eastwood |

With the success of BRUTE!, advertising agencies began to knock on Bennett and Hughes' doors. Big clients such as the Royal Bank of Scotland hired them to produce several one-page ads aimed at the student demographic. Here are some of the best :

226  **BANK-U-THANK!**
228  **BANKER!**
230  **CASH-U-STASH!**
232  **A FISTFUL OF FIVERS!**
233  **THE PROFIT!**
234  **THE HUSTLER!**
236  **SWEET SIXTEEN!**

**APPENDIX!**
241  **THE BIRTH OF *BRUTE!* by Vince Raison**
253  **MORE!**
273  **AUTHORS!**

# PUB ACTION!

Just then, a bloke erupted into the snug with a fiver. The music stopped, jaws dropped and darts hung in mid-air. **'DRINKS ALL ROUND!'** he roared. **'FOR ME!'**

I ran up and kicked him with all I had in the head. Then, I got down on my knees and, butting him in the stonks, tore off his ears.

He screamed when I bit him twice on the eyes and he screamed a whole lot more when I spat them back at him. After that, I ripped out a beer and drank it. Then, when I'd done that, I turned him over and punched his bum in. I bent over and was grabbing his fiver when I saw a note hidden on the deck in front of me: 'Meet me back at the flat for smack and that'.

Panting, I dragged the gleaming, slug-packed **MAC** slowly from its leather harness. After that, I let two dozen slugs into him. Then, I lit a fag, kicked him in the heart a few times and left.

Later, at the address there, I unveil a vicious little Israeli machine pistol and cock it. I counted to one and exploded into the dump.

Six junkies shit for the first time in six months. I smelled the food they hadn't ate. I felt the hate surge through me like a tidal wave of venom. I saw the poverty and wrenched unnaturally.

Just then the gun went off accidently in my hand.

Ugly slugs cut ugly lumps from ugly punks leaving ugly wounds.

I puked up in a pram full of smack.

Next, a bloke sprang into the room with a gun. He pointed it at me. Then he went, 'You've puked on my smack! Take that!' and shot me.

He kept on shooting me till he was out of slugs and that's when I got **MAD!**

I leaned over and, punching my arm up him, grabbed his tongue and quickly pulled him inside out. The sleeve of my Tacchini track suit top was fucked. But it was worth it!

## The End

# THE LAZY BARMAN

Jamie cleared the bar of all its paraphernalia with a sweep of his forearm and lay down. He was the laziest barman in south-east London and he liked a snooze of an afternoon.

He stretched out with a yawn and, dangling one leg over the side of the bar, rested his head on a beer tap and clacked with satisfaction. There was nothing Jamie liked more than doing absolutely nothing. And there was nothing better than a snooze for that!

Just then, a wiry little dog paddled in to the Pub and started panting. Jamie tried to ignore the beast. He was trying to snooze. Then it started sniffing things as well as panting. It was panting and sniffing away without a care in the world and Jamie could hear the clickety-clack of its little feet as it scuttled about. It was hard for a man to sleep amidst all that noise.

'Why don't you just fuck off?!', Jamie said to the dog, telepathically. 'Can't you see I'm trying to sleep up here?!' But the dog just kept on tickering about all over the Pub with its constant sniffing and panting and racket.

Jamie tried to make himself more comfortable on the bar. He was determined to ignore the little dog and to get his afternoon nap like he'd planned. But it was hard to sleep when you're angry, and the little dog was making Jamie good and mad. All he wanted was a lazy snooze but then this little dog barges in and spoils everything. If only the little monster would go away and give him some peace. It was impossible to sleep with all the clatter. But he didn't want to get up and shoo the dog away. He didn't want to do anything. He was the laziest barman in south-east London.

## The End

# BROOKWOOD

**ONCE** upon a time there were three brothers: **ROCKWOOD**, **THUD** and **ELVIS THUG** and they lived in a wood by a brook. Brookwood Estate to be precise.

One day, **ROCKWOOD** was being sick in the brook that ran by the wood when he looked up and saw some men about their job.

**ROCKWOOD** thought, 'What's up?' and went over. 'Where's the foreman, lad?' **ROCKWOOD** said, politely.

'In the pub with your kid, **THUD**.'

'Cor, our **THUD** with a **PINT**!' roared **ROCKWOOD**, rushing off.

**AT** the pub, **THUD THUG** and foreman **BUD THUMP** had a chat.

**BUD THUMP** looked at **THUD THUG** and said, 'Ay, **THUD**!'

'Wha'?!'

'Are you looking at my **PINT?!**'

'**BURP!!! YEAH!** And it's your round,' replied **THUD** brutally. 'I've sucked mine dry like an old bag's **TWAT**! And that's **OFFICIAL**!'

'**OFFICIAL**!' said **BUD**. 'But what about your kid, **ELVIS**? The site is short of muscle and needs good lads like him. But not that **ROCKWOOD** twat. He's as daft as a tap!'

Then **ROCKWOOD** burst into the pub!

'Cor, a **PINT**! I'll have that, mate!' barked **ROCKWOOD THUG**, laughing.

'That's our kid', chuckled **THUD** as **ROCKWOOD** ploughed into the barmaid. 'He's a good 'un!'

**THAT** night, **ELVIS THUG** and his computa bird **DOT BLOCK** were sat by the road laughing at traffic when **ELVIS** said, 'I love you, but you're a hag at that what with all that snot on your snout like that.'

'**MUCK OFF, GRID SLOBS!**' bellowed a passing truck driver.

'Why don't you put a bog around that gob of yours, you ugly sack of pig!?'

'**BUTTON YER LIP, BURGER BRAIN**, and get me down the **PUB**!'

'**BOG OFF, SMOG SUCKERS!**' roared a Jag.

**BACK** at the 'Spud and Borstal', **THUD THUG** was going mad!

'Ay! Did you spill my **PINT**?!!!'

'Where's me kecks?' burped **ROCKWOOD** from the deck.

'Who's been looking at my **PINT**?!!!', foreman **BUD THUMP** said again.

''Ere, **PAT** love, top up his **PINT** and give it here!' demanded **ROCKWOOD**.

''Ere's your **ELVIS** with a car-crash of a gash, lads, and what a monster at that!'

| | |
|---|---|
| Barman: | 'You can't park your car in here, mate. Especially a crashed car at that!' |
| Pub: | **'HA! HA!'** |
| Elvis: | 'You can't talk to my bird like that, you odious beer bug!' |
| Dot: | 'Here's my cash!' |
| Elvis: | 'Yoink! A **TENNA**!' |
| Rockwood: | 'Mine's a PINT!' |
| Thud: | 'Did you spill my **PINT**?!!' |
| Rockwood: | '**BURP**!! **YEAH**!! Down me neck! Get 'em in!' |
| Bud Thump: | 'Ay! **ELVIS**, do you want a few bob for six months graft?' |
| Elvis: | 'What for? She's loaded!' |
| Dot: | 'Get 'em in, **ELVIS**.' |
| Thud: | '**YOW**! Another **FIVA**!!' |
| Rockwood: | 'I spilt his **PINT**!' |

And all was good on the Brookwood Estate.

# OFFICIAL!

# THE CALL

Let me tell you the story of Wild Kid Wallasey and how he was in a pub when he got The Call. (Here I could tell you of how he drove his starving, snow-splattered dog team across the vast, deathlike wastes of Alaska; sailed and single-handedly navigated the treacherous Force Ten storms of the Oceans; clawed and fought his way up the sides of massive, wind-battered mountains; and how, without food, sleep, sweat or beer, crossed the burning, lifeless desert; wrestled live things to the ground with his own hands, captured an entire city and conquered one million squirming teenage nubiles. But it would take an entire hardback to describe his incredible adventure, so, to save you all the boring details, in the end he died).

## The End

# BLOKE-U-POKE!

Rock Buttock was a slut.

One day, when he was in Greaseby Bum Baths, a bloke saw his backeye. He said, 'That's a fine looking shit chute you've got there, Rock. You could make a mint with your hole. Giz a go!'

'Okay,' said Rock, openly.

'Good!' said the bloke. 'Get your farting gear round **THIS!!!**' Then, hastily, the bloke shot his fist into Rock Buttock's bottom and wrenched it out again. Then, he blasted in another. When he punched his arm in again, he ripped out a pipe. A windpipe.

'Sorry,' the bloke said, putting it back.

'Forget it,' said Rock, grimacing.

## The End

# JIM!

It was one of those bleak, black, stormy nights that night as Old Jim hobbled down the coastal road that led to the roaring log fire of the Smugglers Tug Tavern. Above the thundering rain he could hear the merry shouts of laughter which stopped as he burst through the door. 'Evening, Jim,' the pub groaned.

Old Jim settled by the roaring log fire with his jug and lit his pipe. For a while he puffed contentedly until, at last, he spoke. 'Ah-hah! Have I ever told you the one about the time I was press ganged and made Cap'n of the Flying Whippet shortly before we were sunk by pirates and washed up on a beautiful desert island where we were brought back to life and worshipped as gods by thousands of ripe natives who we exploited ruthlessly for all their precious minerals before losing the lot in a poker game with a blind bloke?'
'Yeah.'

**WHEN** I got to the dump I was coshed. Pissed. Plastered. It was the drink.

I pitched out the Jag and piped the dump.

Squat. I aimed at the gaping hole of the doorway and headed for it.

Inside I stopped. Tearing back the mac, I wrenched a gleaming automatic shotgun from the leather harness strapped to my thigh.

**WHOOF!** A monster! I thrust its brutal snout into the dark of the hall.

Me, I can't stand poverty. With some people it's drunks. With me it's poor people. It's the smell: it makes me sick. This dump made me sick. It stank. Real bad. I nursed the hulking muzzle of the shotgun toward the foot of the stairs. I raced up them to the top.

Noise. Lights. Voices. People.

I checked the mechanism on the steel brute in my hands and tore into the first room. A mohican copped it first. The shot blasted him clear across the room.

The next punk backed. I let him. He saw the weapon. He saw its clean, broad snout. He saw the savage flared nostrils of the death hog aimed at his belly. He clenched his teeth, shut his eyes. I hissed. He shit. I squeezed the trigger. The shotgun's fatal bark blew his back out. As he bounced and crumpled I whirled.

Punk three.

I was daft. He moved as I fired. I caught him on the hip. He went down, ruined. The wound lay blasted and raw against his black clothes like a steak in an undertaker's window. He spurted, splashing my Armani jacket near the cuff.

'**CATCH!**' I roared and, leaning over, let the gun shout in his ear. The Armani was fucked.

I knew there'd be panic in the other room. There was, and lots of it. Dopes stood plastered to every corner. As if they could hide from the brute!

A runt in the far corner moved. 'Ay, you!' I thundered. 'Glue bag! Over 'ere!'. I got a grip of his neck and dug in hard. My forehead ground into his. The hog nuzzled his throat.

It was violent. It was brutal. It was savage, vicious and inhuman. But it was fair. I bit him. Then again. He yelled. Then he yelled some more. I bit his nose and chin. I snapped at his lips and ears. I was like a wolf. Besides, blowing holes in people gets boring.

I stopped for a breather. The kid howled so I dropped him. One of the other kids, a bearded boho type in a cap, inched forward.

I grabbed him. 'Where's the dope?!'

'It's behind you!'

I know what you're thinking. You're thinking: I bet he'll turn his back. You'd be right! I did. **THWACK!** The top of my nut caved in and my brain fell out. They kicked it. Then they kicked me in the clothes.

I sank back as another kick pounded my skull. **BOOM!** The gun went off blinding me but I saw the kid drop, a hole gouged out of him.

I'd never fall for that one again.

## The End

# SHOOT!

The day of the big match gangling centre-forward, Stanley Blade, looked at his kit in the mirror. 'MUM!' he roared. 'MUM!'

'You're all right, son,' soothed Coach Hyre, holding his balls in a bag. 'I'm your mum now.'

'But, Coach!' he wailed. 'I've shot me bottle, guv! I'm frightened of football!'

'Scared of sport?!' paled the plimsoll-mad pensioner. 'Are you mad, lad?!'

Just then the ref roamed up and went, 'Three minutes to kick off, Coach. Assemble your lads at the punch line.'

'Right, ref,' he waved, turning on Stan brutally. 'Listen! You can't back out now, kid. I've raised you from the worm you were to the promising young newcomer you are today. You should be over the moon and you will be if you don't get on that field and kick-off!'

Booting a ball before him, Blade pulled up on the pitch as the whistle went for kick-off. Suddenly, he had the ball at his foot and an open goal before him. He surged toward it, the blood racing in his ears, the wind roaring through him. He aimed. The crowd gasped. He pulled back his boot to score...

Just then, Leonardo da Vinci woke up in the Renaissance Arms and sighed. It had all just been a cruel dream.

## The End

# FRANK!

It was cold. Icebergs are like that. I was cold. I lived on one. Alone. But then, I've always been alone...

It all started when I woke up in the Lab and saw this hunchback laughing at me. I knew then that things were bad. Then, when I found a mirror, it was worse.

I was eight-foot-four in me diving boots, green, and had a bolt through me neck. When I came out of the dole people would run up and shout, 'That's my leg!' or, 'That's our kid's head you've got!' and things like that. It was embarrassing. It was true.

They all hated me. All of them, that is, but her. She was just a kid. She played with me. I let her. I killed her. Bad move, when you look like me.

Afterwards, I painstakingly rambled over to Germany to see me Dad, the Doc. He said, 'What's up, son?'

'I am. I'm twenty-eight blokes, Dad,' I slobbered, handing him a sack of bits. 'Make us a bird.'

'Not now, son,' Dad said, sewing a dick on my forehead. 'You're leaving.'

That's when he dumped me on this iceberg. Still, I get to eat fish twelve times a day and all the ice I can suck.

**The End**

# WHEN MORNING WAS OVER

It was eight o'clock Monday morning and the factory hooter was blowing off. A thin mist was clearing over the rooftops of Greaseby as the first drops of rain fell earthward. In the doorway of a derelict pub, Joe shivered and pulled the Harrington up around his neck. In five more minutes there would be no going back.

Joe dragged deep on his cigarette and watched the drizzle wet the narrow cobbled streets that led to the factory gates. He hated this place. It'd been like a prison to him and he'd served his time waiting for the courage to escape. And now he had it and, in just a few more minutes, he would prove it.

He flicked his cigarette into the gutter as Harry Shipright pedalled furiously into view.

'Mornin', Joe,' he called. 'Not going in today?'

'No, mate,' said Joe, defiantly. 'I'm gonna rob the wages van.'

'Give over, yer young bastard,' laughed Harry, cycling past. 'You'll be late, n'all.'

Joe lit another cigarette as the drizzle became a downpour. He trembled, cursing his luck. It would have to rain, today of all days, the day he was ready to break out.

Suddenly, a small green Morris van turned ponderously into the street. Joe stepped forward from the pavement and flagged it down. This was it. He couldn't stop now. His heart leapt wildly as the van shuddered to a halt.

'What's up, Joe?' asked Old Man Johnstone, poking his head through the open window. 'Need a lift?'

Joe wanted to turn and run but it was too late. He snapped into action. 'Yes please, Mr Johnstone. The hooter's already gone.'

'I don't know. You young 'uns,' chuckled Johnstone, opening the passenger door. Joe ducked into the car and, pulling a sawn-off shotgun from beneath his jacket, slammed the door.

'I'm sorry, Mr Johnstone,' Joe smiled, pulling the trigger. Then Joe leaned over the seat and, grabbing the cash box, ran. He knew he would never be able to stop but he didn't care.

He was out.

He was free.

# The End

# THE THING!

I woke up. She grabbed me. 'You bastard,' she hissed. 'Touch me!' Her slit of a gob was cold and wet. Like a dog's snout. Her mad black eyes burned in a neurotic fever. Like a cat. She kissed me with all untamed warmth of a fish. '**KISS ME! KISS ME!**' she screamed. '**HURT ME! HATE ME!**' I did both. She punched me. Hard. I liked it. I grabbed her neck. She came on. 'Get **BACK!**' I barked. She slid beneath me. Hands pulling. Searching. Nails like nails. Cutting. Digging.

The lights snapped on. 'You **TWAT, DAD!**' Vince spluttered. Blood rushed to his head like a football. His fierce eyes scorched by love. He was mad. 'That's my bird **PAT** you've shagged!' He meant it. Every word of it. I was trapped. Like a rat.

The gat appeared from nowhere. I watched it. I shit. 'The slut,' I thought. 'The filthy slut!'

I heard the thunder. **THUD!**
**BLACKOUT!**

## The End

# THE PIG FARMER AND THE BOY

'You been looking at that there pig for a mighty long time there, boy.'

'I sho' have, mister. That there pig is the biggest goddam hog I ever saw.'

'You wanna be careful there, boy. Otherwise you'll be growing into a goddam hog like that yourself one of these days.'

'Like that, you mean, mister?'

'That's right, boy. Just like your father there. That man is jes' the biggest goddam hog I ever saw.'

## The End

# HOLE AHOY!

She came aboard at Liverpool. I saw her straight away. The white flesh of her breasts nudged past me as she made her way to her cabin.

I was young, hard and full of meat and she was the first woman I'd seen in four years.

Later that night, we put out for the Cape and nothing was seen of our passenger for the next two months.

Next thing I knew I was hot, wet and on deck – so was she! From the poop I could see her bending over the rail, the wind flattening her skirt against the curves of her buttocks and thighs. My sheath tightened.

Fore and aft the men began to fight.

Just then, the Cap'n rushed on deck and fired his pistol into a bloke. '**AVAST!**' he raged. '**BELAY THERE, SHIP SHITE! THERE'S ONLY ONE TYPE OF SEAMEN I WANT ON THIS DECK AND THAT'S MINE!**'

He turned on me. He seemed ready to kill me, to bite me in half, when suddenly a cry came from aloft.

'**HURRICANE OFF THE PORT BOW, CAP'N!**'

All hands turned as one to see angry black clouds storming on the horizon. Plus! Angry white lightning crackling within them.

'**BRAIL THE SPANKER! ALL HANDS ALOFT!**' roared the Cap'n. '**WENCH! To thy BUNK!**'

The halliards were vasted, the fo'c'sles bolted and the ship made ready for the wind when suddenly the main mast collapsed and squashed the skipper as flat as a mackerel.

All hands went mad.

She leapt from the poop and grabbed me. She pushed me to her cabin and slammed the door. She stood there breathing. We both did. Outside, the waves began to lash the ship. It had begun to get very hot when the front of her dress burst open. For a moment everything seemed still. The crashing of the sea, the thunder in the sails, the rumble of the storm. I could see her eyes. With mine.

'Lady!' I snarled, hardening. 'The Cap'n's dead!'

'So what?' she gasped. 'You're Cap'n now!' With that, she threw her arms around me and slobbered wetly along my neck. I tried to push her off but she bore me back on a bunk.

'Suck me!' she panted. 'There!'

Afterwards, we both lay there and stank.

# The End

# JIM MALLET STRIKES BACK!

The hood jerked a gat at my map!
 I leapt back!
 **BANG!!!**
 **MISSED!** The slug hit a forehead! **SPLAT!**
 I duck the rod and gut him! He hit the deck! Pat Woodhead shrieked, eyes wide in terror!
 'You brute, Mallet! You brute!'
 She was right. I was tough. Tough as a wolf!
 The jerk bled on the mat! Punters piled out! I grabbed the slut!
 'Listen bitch!' I hissed! 'Get me a cab!' She did it!
 Back at her dump: I lit a fag!
 She had hands like joke shop gloves and a gob to match – and she stank! **GOOD!**

## The End

Pug Pugilist pondered paternally as he tastefully turned into the schoolyard and pulled lumpenly to a halt. He'd seen this ambling spread that was Pig High School for Scum many a time as a young tug and he knew it well. He remembered the day that the slagheap had gushed properly through squashing two hundred and twenty-four pupils, Rochdale, and a joke shop. Aye, he'd seen many a lush and brutal sight at this gratuitous hole in yesteryear but now he was here to see his son, Puglet, play football.

Togged-up true to his nature, Pug aimlessly ambled sideways to the gymnasium where the small boys prepared for combat. It was an unnaturally hot day for September and the pitch was as tough as a bloody pub. Without further ado, Pug assembled at the touchline as the kids ran out, their little balls bouncing before them.

'ROAR!' roared Pug, mob-handed. 'Roar and probably shag 'em!'

Just then, a whistle blew off and a surprisingly full-size, bald and unmarried sports mistress colossally blundered across. 'Basically,' the plucky, flesh-heavy teacher jutted. 'We want a clean game.'

Catapulting, Pug plunged into the flagrantly endless profusion of her record-breaking breasts and unleashed a cock-bracing ambush.

Then, he dropped the leg-iron with which he had wrought the fabulous attack and looked down consumptively at the spunky, blood-spattered mistress akimbo.

'Save your breath!' Pug tub-thumped, his lung whistling heroically in the breeze. 'Mine's a stump!'

Confabulated, the distraught literary buff looked up in awe at the forebodingly knuckled forehead that made up the wall of Pug's head.

'Mr P... P... Pugilist,' she stammered presently. 'The boys must be free to play football here without your blatantly industrial-based intimidation. You may look like a crowd, Mr. Pugilist,' she added. 'But you're not a picket line!'

Pug thumbed the running sore that surrounded his neck and released a pathological glance upward. It had started to rain.

# The End

# JOB'S NEW OVERALLS

Job dusted off his overalls and grinned. They were the best darned overalls he'd ever had. They were bright blue with pockets in every place where pockets could possibly be and they had big red letters right across the back that said: **'ARMSTRONG'**. They were the best overalls he'd ever had and Job was making sure he kept them clean.

'I hear this is the first work you've done in seven years, huh, Job?'

Job squinted in the bright midday glare. 'Yup, it is,' he drawled, 'And then again, it ain't.'

Frank took the scruffy, work-dirty Panama from his head and wiped his brow with his forearm. He spat into the dust. 'Looks to me like you're a mite clean for a working man there, Job.'

Job looked down and scrutinised his bright blue overalls. 'Yup!' he danced, delighted. 'Looks to me like I'm as clean as a gizzard in a paper bag and a damn sight drier too! Damned if I ain't!'

Frank glared at the shack beside the petrol pumps. 'C'mon, Job. I'll treat you to a beer.'

Job jumped slightly, the dust swirling lightly around his feet and settling on his sneakers. 'Hail!' went Job. 'Looks to me like I'm gonna have to be a mite careful before I can jest swan right on over there and drink me a beer. Looks to me like my overalls'd be covered in shit before I was even two strides there!'

## The End

# THE GRINDER AND THE WHIRLWIND

Thunk! Click! **PLOP!**
cough!
Thunk! Thump! click!
clap!
'Cliff Thorburn one. Jimmy White to play.'
**THWAACK!!!**
**PLOP! PLOP! PLOP! PLOP!**
**GASP!!!**
cough!
squeaksqueaksqueak
**THWAAACK!!!**
**THUNK! THUNK! THUNK!** Thunk!
 Thunk! Thunk! th – u n k !
click!
rattle!
**PLOP!**
**GASP!!!**
cough!
squeaksqueaksqueak
**THWAAACK!!!**
**SMAAACK!!!**
**PLONK!!!**
**GASP!!!**
**CLAP!!!**
cough!
'Frame to Jimmy White.'

## The End

# VIC!

Before he croaked I gave him the works. Gun. Fist. Foot. Bollocks. The lot. Then I shoved him in a ditch and planted him. 'Happy Christmas, Jim,' I rasped, laughing, and left.

Back in the heap I was feeling pretty crazy. Like I needed a drink bad. I gunned the Thunderbird down to Santa Monica and hit a bar called Harry's.

It was a dump.

Harry was fat. Had two arms, one eye, and a mouth that spat a lot. I was all ready to knock him out when the redhead showed up.

She was six-two in her heels, pale, thin and white-lipped.

She breezed over. Took a slug at the bottle of J.D. and smiled. Jeez, I coulda killed a kid, she was that cute.

She gave me the once over. 'Six-eight. Ugly. Crumpled suit. Low forehead. You must be Vic Bicep. Private Eye.'

I smashed my head, wet my knickers and bit a bar stool on the leg. When I was through with that I took my head off and banged it on the wall.

Later, when it was done, I hit a Tex-Mex chili bar called Gu-Ba's.

It was a dump.

I was into my third bottle when the Feds cruised in. They wore Dakron slacks and jackets, Bakelite hearing aids and a brace of Remmy riot rifles. I didn't think they were kidding when they asked me outside.

But that was five years ago. These days I'm just another convict on Death Row.

Bald. Bummed. And bored.

## The End

Gunter exploded into the barn. 'What in the hail's goin' on here?!'

Suddenly, Bob stopped.

Gunter loomed over the pig and poked it with his foot. 'This here hog's as dead as... as...'

Gunter didn't rightly know what it was as dead as but when he kicked it again he knew that it was dead. 'Is this pig dead?'

Bob turned his back on the pig so as not to meet its eyes. 'I just came in here and there it was. It's like that sometimes. I come in here and there it is.'

'You mean to say that this here pig's been here before?' the Preacher said in astonishment.

'It kinda looks that way, Preacher, though I wouldn't have known it myself if you hadn't a said.'

'Well I'll be gosh-danged and shagged by a bullet-proof mongoose!' Gunter said, looking at Bob. 'I never know'd there was a pig in here before.' Gunter wiped the sweat from his neck and hitching up his duds, saw a bottle between Bob's feet. 'Well I'll be a ten-foot racoon, Bob. Ain't that your bottle there?'

'Sure as hail is.'

Gunter took the bottle and drank it. Then he got down and rolled on the pig. The Preacher came over and looked at them. Then he looked at the empty bottle. Beads of sweat erupted on his head like little tiny breasts. Then he looked at the pig again for a long time.

'See anything?' asked Gunter.

'Not much,' sulked the Preacher. 'Just that goddam pig and that there empty bottle what you done gone and emptied.'

'Why, Preacher,' laughed Bob, catapulting to his feet. 'That there ain't the only bottle in this here barn.'

Bob slid a crate from under a bale of straw and took a bottle from it. 'It's all here, Preacher!'

While Bob and the Preacher were drinking from the crate, Gunter got to his feet and looked at the pig. He stood there and looked at it for a long time. Then he leapt back.

'Did you see that pig move just then?!' he shouted, startled.

'Not much,' said Bob. 'Here, here's a bottle that's nearly full.'

Gunter looked at the pig. There was nothing much to see but the flesh. There was the snout and the trotters and the tail but, apart from that, it was mostly just like any other pig. Yet still Gunter gazed at the hog as if he'd never seen one in his whole life.

The Preacher turned round and kicked Gunter in the back. 'Why don't you move over and give a man of the cloth a look?!'

'See anything?' Bob laughed.

The Preacher said nothing. Instead, he pulled the stopper from a fresh bottle and emptied it. Then he wiped the snot from his nose with a spare finger. After that he didn't do nothing much but look at the pig.

'See anything, Preacher?" Bob rolled on his back and creased up with laughter when, suddenly, Gunter erupted.

'I swear to God I just seen that goddam pig move!'

Bob froze and, handing Gunter a bottle, stood up to take a look. After he'd finished, he drank another bottle and broke the empty on the pig's head. 'That there pig's as dead as... as...' Bob didn't know just what it was as dead as but he knew it was dead. 'It ain't nothing much but a dead pig anyhow.'

Gunter opened another bottle. 'I knows it's bound to look just like it did the last time but I just can't stop looking at that dead pig.'

The Preacher began to pace nervously around the barn. He didn't stop until he was close to God. 'Don't gawk so! You'd better let a man of God take a look once in a while.'

Gunter fell over, bottleless. 'Sure is damned hot,' he drawled. 'Makes a man wanna empty bottles all day long.'

'Sweet Jesus,' gasped the Preacher. 'I don't know nothing I like looking at more than a dead pig. Just like that one there.' Then, he adjusted his eye to check.

Just then Gunter catapulted to his feet. 'I've got a dong on me that'd choke a three-ton muskrat!'

'Quit yakkin' on so, Gunter,' Bob spat, disgusted. Then he took a Jew's harp from his pocket and began to play.

The Preacher kept time with his feet.

'That there's the best dead pig in the whole world,' roared Gunter. 'Even if it is still alive!'

'That there pig ain't livin' no more'n a lynched cowpoke,' said Bob, removing the harp from his mouth. 'Why, I come down here most every day and there ain't one gosh-danged thing to look at but that there pig. It's the most gosh-danged thing to look at though.'

Gunter fell over again.

'It ain't nuthin' but a dead pig,' Bob went on, laughing. 'But I'll be damned if it ain't just the most interesting thing. You kinda just glance at it and then, before you even know'd it, you can't take your eyes off it. Even if it don't move none, you just don't wanna take your eyes off it.'

Bob put the Jew's harp back in his mouth and began to play. After a while he was playing like he was crazed and there weren't no stopping him until God gave him his last breath.

Gunter was drinking as much as he could manage of anything he found. But he couldn't take his eyes off the pig. Every once in a while he'd jump to his feet and swear the pig had moved or whistled or rolled a cigarette or something. But it was always while the others weren't watching and they didn't believe him.

'Look at old Gunter there,' the Preacher shouted. 'He just can't get his eyes off that pig!' Then the Preacher kicked Gunter heavily in the ribs. 'Shove off Gunter,' he boomed. 'Let the eye of God get in there a while.'

Just then Gunter began to cry. 'I could look at that there pig till I died. There's something about that pig that makes me wanna... wanna...' Gunter didn't rightly know what it was that he wanted, only that he didn't know what it was. But, he consoled himself, at least it was something.

Bob was playing like Satan himself. He was twanging away till he was near dead but he just could not stop. Finally, his finger fell off and the barn filled up with silence.

Gunter began to cry again. 'If I could just look at that there pig 'nd it was a woman I reckon I'd be... be...' Gunter didn't rightly know what he'd be, only that he'd be something.

## The End

# TWIX!

Brenda yawned and stretched, the Alpine magnificence of her breasts looming hugely in the moonlight. She glanced at herself in the mirror noticing for the first time the jutting immensity of her teenage bosoms. Slowly, she began to knead them roughly until two eager nipples sprang out. She groaned and writhed damply on the bed. 'I need a **WANK!!!**'

She began to squirm noisily, her thighs rubbing together, her hands bruising the astronomical proportions of her clitoris.

She slipped a fat log of chocolate between her hot, wet lips. 'Mmmm,' she roared. 'That feels good. There's nothing like the taste of choc to make a woman want to spread out and **WANK!!!**

## OFFICIAL!

# THE PARABLE

'This is a fish!' spat Christ.
'Giz it!' roared the mob.
'Listen!' he said, his wallet billowing heroically in the breeze. 'There was a job. And unto it came lads in their millions. And they said unto it, '**HUH!**''

**Suddenly, there was a plague!
So. There was just one job and God got it.**

## The End

# THE DIARY OF A DEVELOPING WEREWOLF

It all started when I was a pup...

May 29th:
Full moon. Stayed in shaving. Running out of blades fast!

May 30th:
Barked!

## The End

# GREASEBY

At two in the morning on September twenty-first precisely, Jack Hammer sagged into his twenty-third pint at the bar of the Ale Strangler on Lager Lane.

He and Noska had managed, by murderous methods, to wangle the night out together and, not being the type of lads for the peace and quiet of some mere café, had plumped for the illegal after-hours session at the infamous Ale Strangler. Noska had a mate that he'd robbed a lot of money from so dosh was no problem. However, there were other drawbacks...

'Oi!' Jack jeered and, urinating where he stood, ordered four more lagers. Each. 'How come der's no talent in dis dump?!'

'All de best ones are shagging right now,' Noska sulked, ordering another half dozen pints. 'It's two-thirty in the morning.'

Jack watched a fight in the corner and was glad that they'd gone out but the shortage of women bothered him. So, it was with some relief that they annihilated their ale and left.

The rest of the night was just as frustrating and it was with sheer relief that Jack paid the fiver for a gobble from an old bag on the promenade.

Suddenly, a copper appeared from out of the blue. 'I think I'm right in saying,' he said, 'that you are gobbling that man.'

'No,' said the old bag.

'Why not?' Noska yelled loudly and head-butted the old bag on the nose.

'That was brave, lad,' said the copper. 'What made you do it?'

'Well,' said Noska. 'I thought I might put my foot in it, but then I decided to use my head.'

'Very bright,' said the copper. 'Very bright indeed.'

# The End

# THE WILD WEST

**BANG!!!**
    Gunshot!
**BANG!!! BANG!!!**
    Two shots.
**BANG!!! BANG!!! BANG!!!**
    'Your gun's empty, Ringo. Get out of town!'
    'Nope!'

## The End

# THE VIKINGS!

Meat on the table. Women dancing. Tankards bursting with ale. The smell of roasting meat. The sound of a thousand voices raised in song. The taste of victory in every mouth. **VIKINGS!**

Chief Thor Hammer the Mad quaffed back a horn of Nordic proportions and punched a Swede in the head. He surged to his feet, a powerful oath on his lips: '**WENCH!!!**' he roared. 'A horn of Bjornbörger for a Viking Warlord!'

Suddenly, from amongst the Northern Horde, a leather-clad warrior lurched boldly to his feet. 'Raiders!' he cried, his long blonde hair on his head. 'I be chief Orsonberg the Official from the Fjord Estate. Raise with me your horns in honour of our leader in battle this day, the great War Chieftan Thor Hammer the Mad, who has laid on all our beer and **SKÜT!**'

The mighty, blood-spattered Vikings roared their approval and punched each other.

Thor Hammer the Mad threw back his head and howled: 'Today we have won a great victory for the Viking race! We have burst the Brits! Slashed the Saxons! Punched the Picts! Robbed the Romans and gobbed the Gauls!!!'

Just then, Eric the Red walked in and said casually, 'Guess what I've just found?!'

'**WHAT?!!!**' roared the wolf pack.

'America.'

'**YOINKS!!!**' roared the wolf pack again, their horns aloft. '**SKÜT!!!**'

**The End**

# THE EARTH AND THE SOIL

It'd been four years since the last rain and Wolfgang now surveyed his land. For a thousand acres it spread before him: dry, barren, lifeless. The sun beat heavy upon him from its scorching blue ocean.

Wolfgang shifted in the dust and made his way back to the shack. He'd been on this land for twenty-four years. He'd fought Indians, range warriors and governments but nothing could drive Wolfgang from the land his father had died for. Nothing, that is, except drought.

Ute had packed her bag early in the morning. She couldn't sleep. The unbearable heat and the knowledge of their leaving had kept her awake. She'd busied herself with woman's things.

'Tis time, woman.'
'Aye.'
They stood for some time in the door, looking back.
Times.
Aye . . .

* * * * *

Two years later Wolfgang was nicely settled in a small town north of the desert. He had a job as mechanic in a garage and Wolfgang thrived at the chance to blacken his hands.

Ute, too, was happy. For Ute was with child. Daily, she bustled about the hut that they rented from the garage owner with an unnatural velocity.

Wolfgang had crafted a small cot from an orange box and Ute saw to it that the straw was fresh every day. She did it because of her nerves. But Wolfgang didn't mind. 'If she be happy,' thought he, 'then so be I.'

The day Ute had the baby Wolfgang had been working on one of the new model Fords at the garage. The owner was a plump wealthyman with a cheery red face and bright sparkling eyes. He seemed very pleased at Wolfgang's joy.

"Tis a fine stout lad the wife has had then, Wolf?'

'Aye, sir. A farmer!'

The fat man stared at Wolfgang's hare lip, his withered arm. 'I be pleased for thee, Wolfgang lad. For I know that thou dost love thy wife very much. But tell me, wouldst it not be sinful to raise the lad in that oily little hut that thou dost inhabit?'

'I've not given it much thought, sire. To be true, I canst think of naught but motors.'

'Aye lad, I know it. But thou must always remember, Wolfgang, you can't beat the **POTATO!**'

**OFFICIAL!**

# PICK-UP!

Dick Champion ran a bath and got in it.

'**WASH!**' he roared to himself.

Later, he saw himself in a mirror. He was slick, stiff and hard. He rubbed himself with a shirt. '**CHRIST!**' he went. '**I'm not POSH!**' Which was tight really because he'd always wanted a class bird to squirt...

Debbie Tracy had a job in Skyplunge Executive Parking but at night she was different. She had fashion. She had hairspray. She had make-up.

Later, she drooled at a bloke in a mag and wept. 'I wish I was **POSH!**' she whimpered. Which was tight really, because she'd often wondered if she'd ever get squirted by a rich bloke...

\* \* \* \* \*

That night, at the Pub n'Club, there were a lot of Yobs. They drank. They shouted. They did both. When a bird came in they went, '**SNORKYERTWATLUV?!**' and that.

Dick drank a pint. He drank four. Then he saw Cheryl and slid over.

'Shag?!' he announced casually over the **WHAM!**

'Sorry, Dick. I'm on the **BLOB!**' Cheryl roared, tits and fag dangling.

Suddenly, Debbie Tracy raced onto a bus and got there. Her dress was on. Her make-up was, too. She'd had a hair-do. She'd had ten!

She paid the bloke a quid and met a mate. They figged a bit and then lagered. After that her mate, Pat, figured, 'I wouldn't suck a bloke's knob for nowt!'

'I would!' Debs smirked brazenly. 'Twice!'

'**YAK!**' spat Pat. 'Them tonkies taste 'orrible!'

Just then, Dick Champion sauntered back from the bog. Never before had he been reduced to such blagging. He'd asked a bird for a squirt. He'd asked the lot! He felt a fool. Then, he felt another. He was pissed. He was lagered. He was both. But, on hearing a slowy, he made a final heroic effort and plunged wearily back onto the dance-floor.

'Oo, look at that!' directed Pat. Suddenly, Debs knew that here was a man who, she hoped, would, before the night was through, rampantly and without recourse to savagery, squirt her!

**'RUT?!'** Dick asked, his neckwear tightening.

'After,' she replied, hardly figging.

They danced. Then they danced some more. Later, they snogged, cabbed, curried, biffed and squirted.

Next morning she woke up, tasted a tonky, and left.

## The End

# SCAB!

'It's **OFFICIAL!!!** We're **OUT!!!**'

'You're **SACKED!!!**' roared the boss, calling up the cops. '**STOP THAT LOT!!!**'

When I got to the pit it was shut. The route was lined with cops. My mates and me were mad. I ripped out a cosh and barked, '**LADS!!! FIGHT BACK!!!**'

A cop surged forward, picket-punching. I lashed out and dropped him. Then, leaping over his body, I stopped a bus. 'It's the **SCABS** from Job-U-Rob!' I roared, as the cops charged at us. 'Let's get 'em!'

'He's right!' piped a picket. 'Let's burst the bus with bricks!'

'Yeah!' cried another. 'What's a ballot?!'

Then, the lads smashed the cab and, tearing it open, dragged out the scabs. The pigs piled in but we were ready. We'd worked in the dark for this. We were pit-hardened steel and desperate for work. The odds were with us. The people behind us.

But, without the support of any other Union, we lost!

## The End

# BLIZZARD!

It's off with the TV cardies and on with our boots. Aye, it's Yukon weather out there for us to brave for beer and coal and whatever else should come our way this cold and bitter night.

And with a good healthy layer of dirt on our bodies to keep us warm, it's out into the blizzard with packs on backs across the snowy wastelands, boys.

It's no fun, I'm telling you straight, but it's the only work the likes of us can get these days. Struggling through God's snot breaking our backs we are and for what.

## The End

# THE PIG FARMER AND THE BOY - 2

'Note the openings on the female body.'
    'I sure do, Pa. I'm noticing them all.'
    'Well, you'll see them folds of skin around them openings.'
    'I sure do, Pa.'
    'Good. Squat slightly with your legs apart, son.'
    'Like this, Pa?'
    'That's right, son. See, any durn fool can use a tampon.'
    'Even me, Pa?'
    'Even you, son.'

## The End

# P.A.C. MEN!

**WANTED!**
**P.A.C. – MEN!**
The Pub Action Committee
**NEEDS YOU!**
Enrol Today!

Noska lethargically observed the poster in the Job Shop Window. '**PUB ACTION?**' he thought. 'Sounds good.' So he went to the building where auditions were being held. There was a long line of lads when he got there but finally a bloke shouted, 'Next' and it was his go. 'Name?!'

'Noska,' he said, his cap off.

'Address?!'

'Cattle Rock Squat.'

'Age?!'

'Constantly.'

'Right then!' the bloke, a vulturesque fellow with two bright yellow fingers, said. 'We are the Pub Action Committee and we're on the look-out for good war-waging commandos for our squad. We're brutal, messy, cruel and vengeful. But we're fair. We have to be. We're talking **ALCOHOL!**'

Noska snapped to attention.

'Recently,' the bloke continued, 'We've been getting reports of certain people not drinking. If this were ever to get out, for example, to the enemy...' He tapped his substantial nose with a yellow finger.

'My god!' roared Noska. 'Unthinkable!'

'Exactly, my boy! We must get these people away from the

T.V. and **BACK INTO THE PUBS!!!** Are you with us lad?!'
'Aye!' he said, grabbing a pen. 'Let's make it **OFFICIAL!**'

* * * * *

**Madge and Arthur Scroggley were sitting watching 'Win the Wife' after their supper. He was a night watchman on day shifts. She was a pensioner on Mogadon.**

'Our Noska's late tonight, luv,' creaked Arthur, eyes fixed to the telly.

'Probably out with his mates,' Madge sighed, knitting.

**A PINT!**

Noska's neck pumped as he sat crouched and ready in the back of the van. Around him were sixteen of his mates: hand-picked, tough and dedicated to the spread of Worldwide Alcoholism. He'd often heard of people not drinking. Even his father, a man close to his heart, had sometimes refrained from drinking the Hallowed Mead. If ever the lads were to find out...
'Right men!' barked the Squad Commander, resplendent in his Kronenbourg Combat Kit. 'Let's get out there! If anyone resists, subdue him and administer this!' He lifted a half-gallon flagon. 'This is pure spirit, Gold Label and scrumpy! After that they'll be racing you to the Ale Strangler!'

With that, the PAC-men burst out of the van and down the street, breaking off into packs of two to knock at slackers' doors.

Noska and his mate caught a mob of squatters who put up a good fight until they were subdued and put to the flagon. Soon, just as the Commander had said, they put on their ceremonial Blackthorn Aprons and disappeared in the direction of the Pub.

Job done, the two heroes ambled back to the van where a crowd had gathered around an old couple.

'These two buggers refuse to drink!' growled a PAC-man, gripping the old man by the neck. 'They will be interned in a Toxification Camp until their blood count returns to normal!'

As Noska drew up, a wave of fear and compassion washed over him as he recognised the pensioners in question.

'Mum! Dad!' he croaked. '**OH, NO!**'

Noska's parents were later committed to a new 24-hr TV wing at the centre while he was jailed for conspiring with known health freaks.

## The End

# THE FIGHT!

**The mob piled in. Heat. Sweat. Noise. Smoke. The FIGHT! Stripped to the waist they clashed. Local lads locked in combat!**

Mallet spat blood, trod back, ducked and blasted into Gunter's neck. **THUD!**

Gunter took it and roared back like a tank!

**THUD! CRUNCH! SMACK!**

Mallet hit the deck! **SPLAT!**

Mallet snored! **ZZZZ**. **DING!** Saved by the bell!

A wet rag slapped his map. 'Come on kid!' barked his boss. 'We need that cash for meat and that! Do 'im!'

Mallet launched a brutal attack!

Gunter caught a savage clout.

**THWACK!**

and dropped!

'... Seven ... Eight ... Nine ... **TEN!**'

**OUT!**

And that was that!

# The End

# THE ELECTION

The pig trundled mindlessly into the room. Then, trundled out again...

Meanwhile, on the porch, Gunter was sheltering from the sweltering heat when Sheriff Big Jack McCloud rode up and yelled, 'Howdy, voter!'

'Sure is a fine day for the Lord's heat, Sheriff,' rocked Gunter, jetting a stream of tobacco at the law's horse.

'Why hay thar, pig farmer,' the Sheriff drawled. 'I rode on out here t'make sure y'all gonna vote come Friday.'

'Why I'd jest lurv to Sheriff but I've got a mighty sick pig here needs a spoon-feedin' an' if I leave him for too long I gits to frettin'.'

'Things jest won't be the same without your vote, Gunter,' the Sheriff urged, urgently. 'Seems to me like you should jest pick up that there hawg an' take it into town with you.'

'Can my pig vote, too?'

'Sure can, neighbour. I need all the votes I kin git.'

'No shit?!' went Gunter, astonished. 'I'll do it!'

\* \* \* \* \*

Gunter's battered, black dust-covered Ford rattled down Main Street and jerked violently to a halt. The streets were crammed with ale-strangling Georgia folk gripped in the heat of election fever. Guns went off and the sound of frantic piano playing blasted from the saloon.

Gunter licked his lip and, picking up the stricken pig, bolted through the bat wings into the blood-spattered bar of the Malamute Saloon.

The bar was crammed with cow-punching, whisky-drinking, poker-playing shitkickers. Loose women in scarlet sprawled

profitably on pleasure-seeking politicians and free-spending tin miners staked fortunes on the spin of a crooked roulette wheel.

'My, my,' Gunter thought, sweating. 'I think I'll git me a beer. I sure could drink a whole shitload after all that danged fancy auto-mobilin'.'

Suddenly, the pig brightened when a large scale, wide-spread saloon girl approached them behind the breathtaking view of her colossal, world-beating chests. 'Hi there, voter. Like to buy lil' ol' me a drink?'

'I sure would, Miss,' drawled Gunter, shouldering the pig.

'But I got me here this sick pig needs a suckling but it sure looks to me like you could feed a whole shitload.'

Just then Dangerous Kid Cruelty roamed up usefully. 'No woman o' mine is gonna suckle no goddam sick pig, boy,' he warned, levelling the gaping black tunnel of the six-shooter at Gunter's pig. 'So, git outta here!'

'You can rape ma wife and kids. You can burn ma farm an' chop ma chickens but don't you never point no gun at ma pig,' drooled Gunter. Then, he stepped back and, checking his weight, launched a bloke-stopping poke to the kid's brains and killed him.

'I like a man with spunk!' the saloon girl jutted, territorially. 'Buckets of it. Why don't we go up to my room and fool around?'

'Goddam it, miss, I'd jest lurv to,' Gunter drawled, fingering the pig. 'But I got a mighty sick-looking hawg needs a fondlin' an' if I leave him for too long I gits to frettin'.'

'Why don't y'all jest pick up that there hawg and bring it up with you?'

'You mean ma pig can come, too?'

'Sure can, pig farmer. He's old enough to vote, ain't he?'

'No shit?!' went Gunter, astonished. 'I'll do it!'

# The End

# THE ANGLER!

plop

**The End**

# JOB!

Suddenly, I burst down a long dim-lit door-lined corridor and, exploding into one, erupted into the vast wetness of her limitless breasts and stopped. Hardening, I jabbed the **MAC** into her ribs and spat, **'GET NAKED!'**

We did it.

Just then, Kid Colt burst in. **'GET BACK!'** he barked, twin pistols packed. **'THAT'S MY GASH YOU'VE SNATCHED!'**

**FLASH!!! I ATTACKED!!!**

**BUT!** She stepped back and **CRACK!**

It went black.

\* \* \* \* \*

'Mallet?'

**'WHAT?!'** I asked, arching. Then, I saw her! The sheer vital tonnage of her. I leapt to my feet.

Kid Colt charged in, spurting lead. I copped one in the neck and laughed.

**'YOU'VE MADE ME MAD!'** I roared, wounded.

He'd blown off the lot and his gat was blank when I got him. Jetting, I drove my fist straight through his stomach wall and, grinning, ripped his liver from his body loudly.

**'YOU WON'T BE NEEDING THAT WHERE YOU'RE GOING!'** I spat and, cramming his body into the toilet pan, pulled the chain. Then, **MAC** out, I blasted her. I hit a pub and, laughing, drank it.

**JOB DONE!**

# The End

# MUGVILLE

When I got there they were sleeping. All but Kid Pensioner. He came over and said, 'This is a two horse town, son. And I'm both!'

I took his word for it, and left.

## The End

# THE REBEL

**Ivy strained the fat from the custard and sighed. It was the Lord's fourth portion that morning and she was bored. When she first got her job with God she'd been really excited but now, after 320 years, her heart had begun to pine for the men of a shipyard or barracks.**

'Ivy…? Ivy…? Iveee?'

She tutted and, casting a casual glance at her untouched lager, picked herself up.

'Here you are, God,' she said, placing the pudding before him.

'Cheers, Ivy love,' God blessed heartily. 'Yer a cracker, even if I did make you meself.'

Ivy blushed and tried to cover her two massive wet breasts with two tiny dry hands.

'Give over, God,' she giggled.

''Ere,' God got serious and, turning down the sound on the television, forgave the custard for a cigarette. 'Where's that bloody Jesus, then?!'

'God knows.'

Just then, God moved in a mysterious way. 'What's got into that lad? He's out all the hours I send!'

Suddenly, Jesus flew in. 'Hi, Dad,' he landed.

'Where the bloody hell have you been?!' asked God.

'Look, I'm sick of your holier-than-thou attitude!' Jesus flapped. 'There was a stay-behind in The Wilderness so some Romans put me up for the night. Anyway, I'm off to The Last Supper for a pint with the lads.'

The Lord mumbled and pulled out a sack. 'God's speed?'

'Thanks Dad. I'll need it!'

**SNORT!!!**

# The End

# WORMWOOD

Once upon a pint there was a dump called Wormwood and **ELVIS, THUD** and **ROCKWOOD THUG** were in it. Suddenly, they escaped but were grassed, framed, trapped, set up, bribed, bummed and banged up again.

**ONE** day, **THUD THUG** was on the bog exercising when Officer Droppam burst in. 'Oi!' he screamed, confidentially. 'Your kid **ROCKWOOD** is going gay!'

'**YOINKS!**' roared Thud, attractively. 'Our kid a fag!'

'That's right. So fill your pot and get 'im!'

Meanwhile, on Z-wing, **ELVIS THUG** and **BOX DUPALOTT** were laughing at nowt when Mac le Beast roamed up. 'Need a fist-fuck, chuck?' he said, in French.

'Not now. Not never. Not with you. No,' rasped **BOX**.

'Yeah, beat it,' spat **ELVIS**.

'Ah, come on, fellas,' pled Mac le Beast. 'Give a cock a home.'

'I wouldn't give your cock a biscuit,' barked **BOX**. 'I wouldn't give your cock the pleasure of savage brutality!'

'Me, neither,' slurred **ELVIS** in his characteristically Bavarian accent that amazed felons and fugitives alike. 'So fuck off!'

'You think you are sole good with your tight little bottoms and your Viking manners. So why don't you sit on the toilet? Why don't you play your draughts and dominoes? I know plenty that would like a good bum punch! That **ROCKWOOD** twat for one!'

'Are you calling his kid a turd burglar?' **BOX** burst.

'Oui.'

'You're a fucking liar,' **ELVIS** tightened unnaturally. He felt the heat of the gas burn on his neck. He smelt the smell of a thousand stinking pots. He heard the inhuman cries of five thousand condemned men. He tasted the beer that wasn't there. He saw the sweaty, frightened face of Mac le Beast and laughed. 'Prove it!'

'You bet I can. Zis morning zat Chinese kid, Bum Funn Chum, sez 'e was in your bruzzer only las' night.'

Just then, **THUD THUG** rushed up fast and stopped. Panting, he gasped, 'It's **OFFICIAL!** He's a glove puppet! Our **ROCKWOOD** is bent!'

That night, at slop-out, **ROCKWOOD THUG** was in a bloke when Officers Ripemoff, Feelham and Petit and Governors Stripham, Wetham and Shaggam walked miraculously in. 'What's up?!' roared Wetham, his suit on.

'I am! Apparently.' **ROCKWOOD** felt bum-hole-grip-in-fear.

'You've bummed that lad!' Shaggam shouted, his hard on.

'Twice,' laughed **ROCKWOOD THUG**. 'Look!'

'You offal-robbing bum bandit!' spluttered Officer Ripemoff. 'Get your gut off that lad's back!'

Suddenly, **THUD THUG** and **ELVIS THUG** burst out from nowhere accompanied by an intrepid stench.

'What's that on our kid's cock?!'

'The fat lad's bum.'

'A fat lad?! In Wormwood?!'

Just then, Officer Ripemoff got stuck up and went: 'Come on men, there's meat for all. Plenty of it.'

'Yoinks!' howled a screw. 'He's right!'

And that's how the fat lad got bummed flat in Wormwood nick.

**OFFICIAL!!!**

# JOCK!

Bob Jockey was good at sports. All of them. He bagged a cup. He bagged the lot. Back then, Coach Fondle bragged. Said Bob was going places.

'Yeah', Dad laughed, 'McPlaces.'

Bob shot off the sofa and broke the telly. He'd watched a lap. He'd watched plenty. Now, Bob was **MAD!** He snatched a pop and gulped it. Dad was right; Bob had done **NOWT!** He reached back, grabbed flab and farted. At school, he'd been top at 'owt. But pop and crack had done him in. He'd been lapped at the track and laughed off the bus. He'd pissed his own sack.

## The End

# BETWEEN TWO LUNGS

I don't have friends. **GOOD!** Who needs 'em? Not me. The only friend I have is my **MAC** 10. One-point-six kilogrammes of instant death. A beauty. A little too bulky for my pocket, that's true, so at work I house a Browning. A war hog. So, why all the guns? Well, as any D.H.S.S. Fraud Investigator will tell you, it's getting awful rough out there on the streets.

My name's Mallet. Jim Mallet. People who know me call me Mr. Mallet. I'm a plug-ugly gang if ever there was one. When I was a kid, I always wanted a job that'd give me access to other people's homes. True, this job didn't exactly offer the prospect of destroying a lot of exotic locations but it did have its perks. I get to go into any home I want. Lots of them. Like this one.

This one was a squat above a tobacconists on Shepherd's Bush Green. I was after a turd called Firth. Julian Firth, the Bishop's son. He was an actor. A bad one. I say 'was' because when I found him he was dead! He was lying on a badly worn Afghan mat with the syringe still hanging from his arm and a big crowd of cops all around him.

'Who called you, Mallet?!'

It was Ford Stockwood. Detective Sergeant Stockwood, Homicide. We went back a long way. He was as bent and as crooked as they come. Like me.

'What's the dope, Stockwood?!'

'Ah, nuttin'. Kid popped out on junk, see.'

'So what's wiv de murder boys?! Dirty?!'

'Nah. S'all routine stuff. Know 'im?'

'Sure. The stiff's a ham actor called Julian Firth!'

'Actor, huh?'

'Yeah! Y'listenin'?!'

Stockwood rescued the smokes from their cellophane gaol and flashed. Lighting up he says, 'So why you in?'

'Routine! I heard he found a fiver that he never declared! I don't like that!'

'A fiver?'

'Yeah! Y'listenin', aren't yer?!'

'A lousy fiver? You were muscling the kid for a lousy fiver?'

'So what's lousy about a fiver?! I like fivers! I like all I can get! Besides, who's to say he hadn't done it before?! One day it's a fiver, the next it's a grand!'

'Jesus, Mallet. Your job stinks.'

I filled my fists with the cheap man-made fabric of his off-the-peg suit and drove my knees into his ribs. 'Listen, copper!' I hissed. 'I don't have to stand here all day and listen to you bad-mouthing the system! The system **IS** and that's official! You've got your job and I've got mine! My job's to make sure that the scum don't steal off the people! Evasion of income tax is a crime! A vicious crime! A crime that drives our Government into the hands of the international money lenders! If all these punks paid up it'd be another story! And you'd better believe it, Stockwood, when I say I'm here to make them pay! Never forget that!'

I slapped his puffing face with the back of my hand a dozen times or so real fast and then let him have it in the guts. Then I pointed him at the body.

'See that?!' I rasped. 'See that?! That's what dodging the system does for you! How can anyone afford an overdose on three quid a day?! If I could've caught him earlier then maybe he'd still be alive right now!'

I dropped him then and straightened what was left of his suit a bit.

He waved his heavies back with his arm and loosened his tie. There was a gleam of something mad in his eye. 'You're dirty, Mallet. Very dirty. You're as low as they come. Know that? It's you and your likes that drive kids to this.'

'That's crap!' I snarled. 'Rich people take junk, same as anybody! Content yourself with that, sucker! Rich people are as human as you!'

With that, I left. When I hit the street it was raining hard. The tarmac had that yellow glow from the overhead street lamps that I usually write about when I'm looking for atmosphere. The traffic was roaring by. There were people all over.

Poor people!
**GOOD!**

# The End

# NEVER SAY DIE!

Carefully, Jack hurled himself from the cliff brandishing his sabre between his teeth, his tartan headscarf fluttering traditionally in the rushing wind of his rapid descent. He hit the water with a terrifying **SPLASH!**

For a time, the sweaty, black-faced crew of the Sea Eagle stared pop-eyed at the point where Jack had vanished. Seconds passed. Anxious tongues licked thin, cruel lips. The seconds were becoming minutes. Nervous glances charged across the crowded deck like a pack of hunting wolves. Yet still there was no sign of Jack.

"E's gorn!' Hook McFinney broke.

Then, as a whisper stole as lightly as a thief across the deck, the water suddenly split white and Jack gushed upward at the stars for air.

A great roaring cheer rent the location as the crew went mad.

'Jack's back!!!'

## The End

# THE GAMBLER!

'**ALASKA!**' yelled Grit Bunker. 'I've robbed it! Robbed, raped and plundered it! Just now!'

Just then a card sharp shuffled up and went, 'My name's Block. Block Schwerz. An' this here's ma kin, Pat! Notice the Nordic proportions of her voluminous young planets! So, nuggeteer. Cut the deck to win a squeeze of these!'

'Dust for lust, huh?'

Grit looked at Pat. He looked at her eyes. Then he looked at her breasts. He could not take his eyes off her breasts. They wrestled loudly towards him like two eager young seamen.

'Name the game, card crap,' Grit drooled.

Schwerz slithered round and hissed, 'Cut! Highest card gets the lot!'

'What's the stake?!' Grit demanded, his eyes still molesting the buttock-like enormity of her breasts.

'**ALASKA...OR THIS!**' Block roared, wrenching the flimsy, hot threads of her scanty nightie aside to launch the inexhaustible dimensions of her bust upon them.

Grit fought back the rising stench of his manhood and pondered. After sixty-four winters up the Yukon with nothing but wolves to fuck, Grit was ready to **RUT!** Furiously! But he knew that if he lost he would have nothing. Could he risk it all for Pat? After all these years?

But now a crowd had gathered round, intent on seeing Grit lose his gold for grunt. 'Go for it, Grit!' they egged. Grit licked his lips greedily. He could not take his eyes off her breasts.

'I'll do it!'

'**CUT!**' rasped Block Schwerz, holding out the deck.

Grit did it!

'It's a three!' someone gasped.

Grit groaned, feeling his wad wilt instantly.

'I've scooped your loot!' Block Schwerz laughed.

'Shut it and cut!' Grit grinned, ripping out his pistol and leveling it at Block's head. 'And you'd better pray that it's a two!'

It was.

# The End

# ME, SEAMAN

He crushed his mouth across her shivering flesh.
 'Now! Now!' he panted.
 Her broad hips writhed against him. He grabbed her. She arched erotically in his hands. 'Love me,' she gasped. 'Love me hard!'
 Years later, Wolf gazed out across his ship as it went around the world. **'LAND AHOY!'** shouted a bloke in a basket.

The men, hungry for lust after a two-year voyage, fought wildly amongst themselves to get into the boats.

'**AVAST, DECK SWABS!**' roared Wolf, clouting the stern of an eager young seaman. '**PLUNDER!**'

'Come ashore, cap'n!' cried Jack, the cabin boy.

'Not me, lad. I'll not taste the flesh of native women. Not while I search for **HER!**'

That night, by the light of the burning villages, Wolf stood alone on deck. He cast an empty bottle of rum into the water, the sound of his men's bestial revelry floating across the cool air of the bay, horrifically!

Then, catapulting backwards, he bolted the for'ard fo'c'sle and grabbed the mainbrace. '**PAT!**' he cried. '**HOW LONG MUST I WAIT?!**'

Suddenly, the air smelt soft and womanish and the memories came flooding back...

# The End

# THE SUBBUTEO KING

It began!
**FLICK OFF!**
Flick! Flick! Flick!
**FLICK!**
**GOAL!!!**
One-nil!
What a flicker!

## The End

**BRUTE** Thunder stormed at the **PUB!** Mad with hate! Brute was big and tough. Like a truck. And he could prove it! Nobody crossed Brute Thunder without a clout. Not even Jet Outburst and his lot.

**JET** Outburst looked up from his pint in fear. Jet had called Brute a **TWAT!** at work. And now his mob could do nowt! It was Jet and Thunder! Two men! To the death! **OFFICIAL!**

**BRUTE** Thunder burst into the pub with the savage intensity of a **ROCK!** 'OUTBURST! You **TWAT!**' Brute spat. 'I'm no **TWAT!** And that's a fact! Sup that jug and get your gob out 'ere now!'

**JET** piped his mob. Nowt moved. 'You **SCUM!**' he barked. 'I've no need of thee to **THRASH** that **TWAT!** And I'll use **OWT TO DO IT!**' And with that he smashed his mug on a bloke!

**BRUTE** Thunder blasted at Jet Outburst with all the unbridled ferocity of a **WARHEAD!!!**

**BRUTE** blocked a clout but snapped back like a wolf. Jet lashed out a fist of glass. Brute ducked but his snout copped a bit of it.

**JET** butts out. Brute comes back. Now it's Jet! Now it's Brute! Jet cops a blow to the neck, and another and another and Brute's on top! He's driving in punch after punch after sickening punch. **WHACK! WHACK! WHACK! WHACK! CAN JET TAKE IT?! OH!** Brute stumbles and **JET COMES BACK LIKE A PARATROOP ATTACK!** He bites! He **CUTS! HE MAULS! CRACK!** Oh my word... **PUNCH! LEFT! RIGHT! STRAIGHT LEFT! JAB! JAB! UPPERCUT, HOOK! WHAT A SWIPE!!! AND HE'S DOWN! BRUTE THUNDER IS DOWN!!! STAMP! KICK! WHAT A SPANKING! WHAT A POUNDING! THEY'RE AT IT LIKE HAMMERS!!! IT'S A BLOODBATH!!! BUT BRUTE'S BACK! HOW DOES HE DO IT?!!! HA! THIS MAN CAN TAKE OWT! HE'S A BULL! A MONSTER! A FRENZIED, SAVAGE THUG!!! HE'S ROARING LIKE A DOG! HE'S TEARING JET TO PIECES!!! IT'S DISGUSTING!!! AND – THAT'S IT! HIS HEAD GOES IN! JET GOES DOWN! THIS IS THE END! HE'LL DO NOWT AFTER THAT! HIS LIFE'S SPURTING OUT FROM A VERY NASTY WOUND INDEED. BRUTE THUNDER HAS DONE IT!**

**BOOT** atop the body, Brute howled in **VICTORY!** His head all blood he faced the mob! His gob split in a savage snarl! The mob pulled back, their leader dead!

'**I'LL BLOW MY GUNS OFF IF I WANT!**' he screamed. 'And you'll do nowt but listen! I have come here this day and laid waste! This carnage, this bloody slaughter of your mate, Jet Outburst, heralds the end of your wrecking activities!...'

'YOU'RE ABOLISHED!! THIS PUB IS MINE!! And I'll **KILL** to keep it. I'm a one-man fucking slaughterhouse with a thirst for **ACTION!** For devastation, beer and **GRUNT!**

'I can lead you, **LADS!** We can rule the length and breadth of every **PUB IN ENGLAND!!!** For-we-are-**MEN!!! MEN OF ENGLAND!!! AND WE LIVE BY ONE LAW AND ONE LAW ALONE! AND THAT IS THE LAW OF FANG AND CLUB!!! LIVE BY IT OR DIE!!! ARE YOU WITH ME LADS?!!!**'

'OFFICIAL!!!' roared the mob.

## The End

# NO ONE GETS BETWEEN A WOMAN AND HER ICE CREAM

Me mum always warned me not to get between a woman and her ice cream.

But I did.

See, I was in bed when the ice cream van arrived.

I seen her buying a '99. It was just a glimpse of her. But it was enough.

I stormed out onto the balcony. 'Oi! Don't be selling my bird no fucking ice cream, mate!' I yelled.

Instantly, in one spectacular movement, the bloke catapulted into his seat and shot down the street.

'Mmmmm!' went Pat. 'This ice cream's fucking delicious!'

The sun was setting to the south. Dogs were barking. Children were crying. Shoes were in the street.

'Put the ice cream on the ground!' I warned, reaching for a stick. 'And come back into the house with your hands in the air!'

'No,' went Pat, honestly. 'I've got a '99 here and if you know what's good for you, you'll stand back until it's finished.'

I did. After all, me mum always warned me not to get between a woman and her ice cream.

## The End

# QUACK!

My name's Gore. Doc Gore. N.H.S.S. Surgeon. I like guts. I get them. Miles of them.

One day, I cut this bloke's head off for a laugh. His mum went mad. Next, I snatched this kid with a brain tumour. It was great. I wheeled him in for the students.

'**WATCH THIS!**' I roared and went to work. 'After making the initial incision I will cut, hew, hack and slash a bit. Here! Like this!'

The students cheered as I stabbed, sawed, chopped and trimmed. Then I paused and, lighting a fag, shaved, snipped and clipped a bit.

Just then this girl yelled out, 'Ay, mister! Giz a go!' 'Go 'ead!' I laughed. 'Get stuck in!'

She started off with a good old-fashioned two-handed incision. Then she said, 'Mind if I carve, slice and amputate a bit?'

'Sure!' I waved. 'Go 'ead, love. That's a bloody great wound you've made! Carry on! I'm going to the pub for a shit!'

She was really putting her weight into it when I got back. You could tell because the kid woke up. 'Nurse!' I sniggered. 'Cosh that kid will yer!' She did it. Then I pushed her aside and waded into the **NUT**.

Boyishly, I lopped off the end of his knob and trod on it. Then I got down to business. A quick hack and slash. A little peeling, gouging, beheading and that.

Just then, a nurse splashed up and went, 'He's dead, Doctor.'

'Never mind,' I laughed. 'I may have lost a patient, but I've made a fucking great hammock!'

## The End

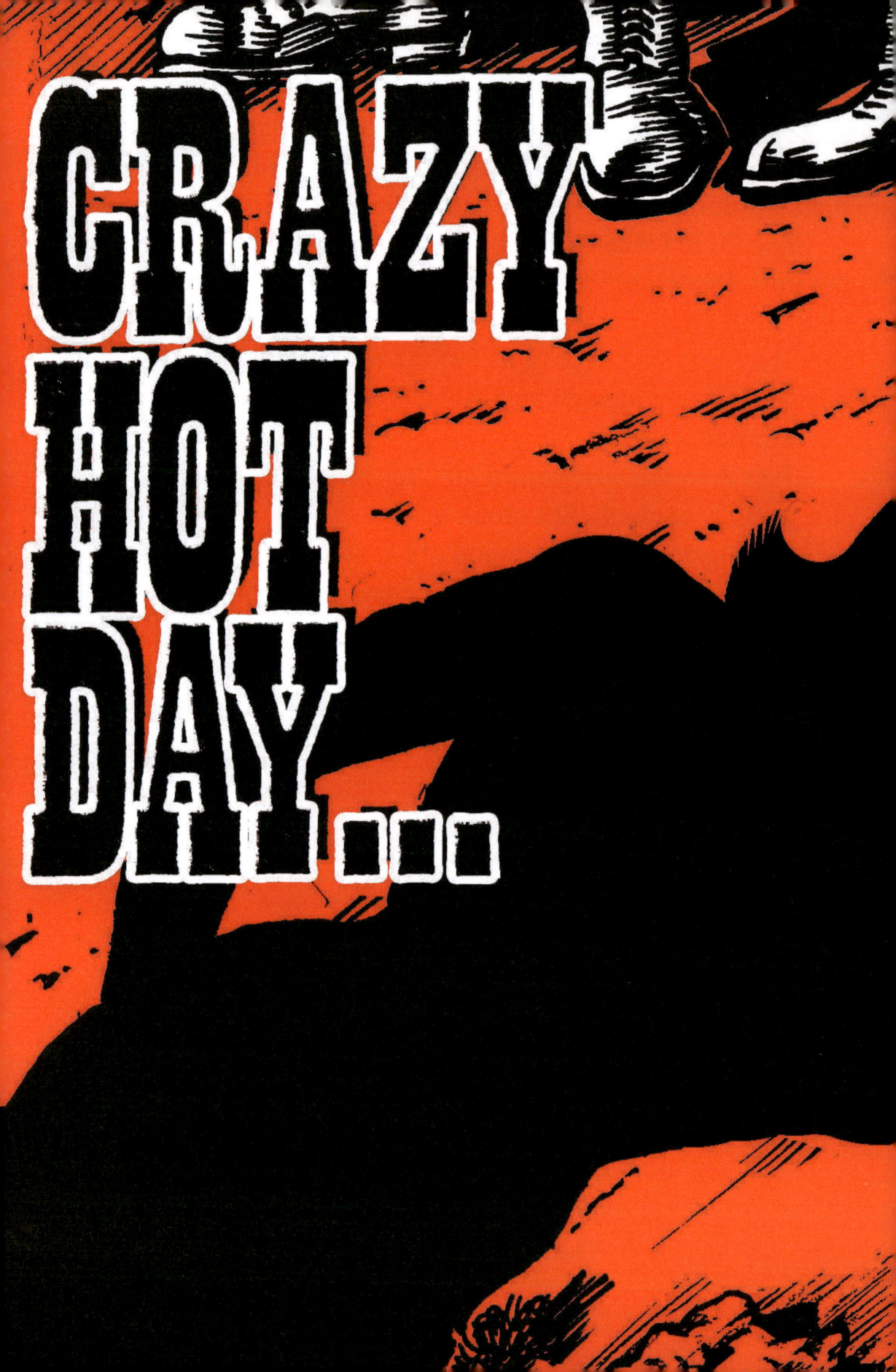

It was one of those crazy hot days. The men were on the sidewalk. They were sweating.
Just then, a bus drove up.
The men watched it.
Then, the bus drove off again.

Rut Landscape watched it go. Rut had had a hard life. He'd only been six years old when he saw his entire family die at the wheel of a locomotive. Later, he'd lost a dick in a bathing accident and it was a wound that had plagued him ever since. Plus, he was hot and lost.

Rut looked away then and drew a frog in the sand with a stick. He was thirsty.

Suddenly, another bus drove up and stopped. A woman got off it and stood looking at the men through the swirling clouds of dust. She could feel the hot sun burning the back of her bare legs.

As one, the men gulped and popped out thick pink tongues that moistened.

She could feel their eyes roaming all over her body, exploring every inch as if she were naked.

Rut clenched convulsively in his pocket. It was Pat!

'Rut Landscape!' she breathed, awesomely.

'Pat Walton!' he gasped. 'Git the hail outta here, Pat Walton! Ain't you broken enough men with your lovin'?!'

The men surged noticeably.

'If I know you, Pat Walton, you're up to no good in that thin, breast-hugging cotton dress.'

'It'll be different this time,' Pat panted. '**LOOK!**'

Then, with an horrific ripping sound, the men erupted in a fit of high-spirited antics.

Rut looked. His jaw dropped and a yard of spittle fell on his shirt. He could feel the hot desert wind dry the sweat on his back. He could taste the dust in his mouth. It was gritty and hot. A tumbleweed blew across the road…then blew back again. The veins in his neck and body stood out heroically. He tried to look away but couldn't. Nervously, he drew a ship in the sand with his stick. He was as puzzled as a possum in a parka.

    By now the men were fighting to look at Pat whose breasts struggled simultaneously to remain within the confines of her thin cotton dress.  When she moved, her naked thighs squeaked together, the sound of which drove the men to fight all the more.

    'I've never cared about that wound of yours, Rut,' she steamed, hotly. "You're the only man that can satisfy a big gal like me!"

    At the sound of that the men suddenly stopped fighting. 'Yeah!' they shouted, throwing their hats in the air. 'But there's ten of us!'

Quickly, Rut drew a fork in the sand with his stick. 'Who in the hail's he, anyways?' one of the men yelled, surging forward. 'Why he ain't no more use than a spotted hog in a goober tree!'

'Yeah!' roared the men. 'Let's lynch him!'

They did it. Then they grabbed Pat.

Later, the last bus drove up and stopped. Pat got on it and left. The men were on the sidewalk. They were sweating. It was one of those crazy hot days.

# The End

# WOLF!

I was watching telly when she called me.

'**WOLF!**' she went. '**WOLF BOXA!**'

My ears pricked back and I whined a bit. But I never went. I'm not soft. I know what old bags want off big dogs like me – and it's not potatoes!

'**WOLF!**' she went again, in her special way. 'Come up here or you won't get your dinner. It's your **PAL!**'

I slobbered and licked my face. When I'd done that, I scratched a bit and padded upstairs to the bedroom. She was all there. Every yard of her!

She loomed up and patted the bed in that special place. 'Come up here, Wolf!' she breathed, sinking back into the pillows. 'There's a good boy. Do what mummy says.' She showed me a bit of meat. I leapt up and ate it but, before I knew it, she'd got me. She made me sprawl all over her. She got underneath me and opened a bag of crisps. I ate them. Then I ate a bar of chocolate. Frankly, I ate everything I could.

She rolled me around on the bed. She stroked my chest and stomach. She scratched behind my ears. My tongue hung out and I waved a leg in the air.

She reached under me and pulled me with her special grip. She was panting and thrashing about like a bitch on heat and I wasn't exactly freezing meself, see. So, I got down there and sniffed, licked and, later, got fed – and I don't mean **POTATOES!**

## The End

# THE PLOT!

**WHACK!!!
I ATTACK!!!**

**The End**

# PUB HAWK!

**Suddenly, Wing Commander Tom Wallasey sprang into the mess. 'IT'S WAR!!!'** he screamed, in upper class.

The men mumbled and stirred in their goggles, their scarves dangling heroically in their beer.

Quickly, I stuffed back a lager field and lurched boldly onto the bar. **'LADS! PIES! PUBS! PINTS!! And SCRAMBLE!!!'**. We did it!

Ten planes took off. Magnificently, we flew them up. While I was driving I ripped out a bottle of scotch, tore the head off, and plugged it in.

**'AAAAH!'** I went. **'COMBAT!'**

When I woke up, there were Fokkers everywhere. **'SHIT!'** I screamed and put my foot down. Lead hit my cockpit. I plunged into a cloud. The Fokkers plunged after me. I dove over Dover, flew over France and landed in London for lunch but I couldn't shake them off. Back in the sky, they were driving around all over the place. Later, I got fed up and crashed.

When I woke up, I was being punched in the headquarters of the German Army. They wanted my name, rank and number. They got them. **FAST!** Then, the one with the beer opened a bag and took out a leg. My leg. I could tell by the cock at the top.

What they did to my other leg is enough to make the hairs in your pint stand up.

# The End

# THE WOLFS

WOLF never wanted to go to art school. He didn't. He went to war. It was a war that killed him. He'd never known the son he'd had.

Wolf Jnr. had never known his dad. Some say it was this that made him the ruthless man he was. For Wolf Jnr. ran slaves from the Barbary Coast to New York. He'd hated the world that had given him the millions he'd died with. But he left his children penniless.

Of the three the youngest, Wolf V, died first. He was two when he coughed up his lungs. His two brothers, Wolf III and Wolf IV, ran away together and signed up with a whaling ship, The Majestic Lance, in Nantucket. It was a voyage in which the beast would kill them both.

Their mother, Sabine, missed them. She wept. She was far too old to bear child. She knew that the family tree had finally been timbered.

Forever.

## The End

# THE LEGEND OF PAUL DIAMOND

Paul Diamond was a girl's best friend – and he knew it! He had a big knob and could go on for hours. He was an athlete. A young god.

Tina Pearson loved fashion. Any fashion. She wore Chelsea Girl tops, read Titbits and listened to Radio One. But she had problems. She couldn't rut!

They met at a stomach-pumping party on the Costa Living in Spain. Henry Cooper presented the first prize of one million pints of Pig Lager to them both.

Suddenly, they'd drunk them!
Paul cast a glance at her gob and belched triumphantly.
'I'm gutted! Fancy a curry?!'

'Not half!' she screamed horrifically, hurling herself backward and exposing herself in mid-air.

'Get naked!!!'

'What kind of girl do you think I am?' she asked, landing loudly.

'Look, I've got a wicket of elephantine proportions and I can go on for hours,' he loomed gloomily.

His eyes looked at hers. Her eyes looked at his. Their eyes looked at each other. It was hot. They were sweating. The sea was coming in... then going out again. In the distance they could hear music. Distant music. They sweated some more. The sand was hot and dry. They were young and drunk. Her mouth was damp and wet. Wet and damp. It was both.

'I have problems with my orgasm!' she gasped. 'I don't have them. I can't! I won't! I never will! **NEVER! NEVER! NEVER! EVER!**' she erupted into a fit of tears and fell into his arms.

'My name is Paul Diamond,' he wavered nostalgically, indicating the agricultural proportions of his swimwear. 'And I'm a girl's best friend.'

It was still hot. Somewhere, a bus went past. A dog barked. A pub opened. They were sweating.

He lowered her to the sand. 'Paul,' she groaned, realistically.

'Yup.'

'Make me come!'

His swimwear wrenched brutally.

She touched him. He touched her. They were touching each other.

'Oh, Paul!' she writhed unnaturally. 'Say you love me! You do love me, don't you?'

His sideboards tightened. He narrowed his eyes into slits. Clenched his fists. His mouth opened wide. His legs bent. His toes knotted.

'Marry me?'

**SQUIRT!!!**

Just then he woke up. He was still on a bus. He was going to work. It was Monday. It was raining. The streets were crammed with people. Wet people. When he woke up again he was at work. He woke up again at the pub. Then, at the match. Finally, he woke up at home.

Tina was sprawling rampantly in her pink baby doll nightdress eating chocolate with her bare hands. There was chocolate on her breasts. On her thighs. There was chocolate on the tap. There was chocolate outside. Beside her, twelve cans of Pig Lager lay crushed next to a damp drainpipe.

Just then, he collapsed in general squalor and roared, 'At least I've still got my memories!'

# The End

# A BROKEN MAN

I was all about done in by the time we got there. Absolutely knackered as a matter of fact.

It was a big old place at that, too. A three storey, red-brick job with a neat whack of paint. One of those lifetime guarantee I.C.I. jobs by the look of it. There wasn't a crack in it. Did the place proud. All the same, I was quite excited. It was a definite crawl toward the middle classes this dump. Wall-to-wall labour-saving devices. Pine kitchen. Microwave. Seven-foot-thick Axminster shag pile. Salvador Dali furniture. David Hockney. Brown sugar. Everything one had always wanted. Even the Guardian. It took me about half an hour to do the path.

At the door, Bradford did the chat. It was his 'touch'. I lingered at the steps, panting. Done over double I was. They thought I was in a fine mess. We were invited in. I made Bradford help me through the door.

'You look like death, mate!' he said, casing the joint. I should do at that, I thought. I was doing my best.

By the time we'd made it through the shag pile to the kitchen I was a sweating mass. There was no stopping me. It pissed out all over the show. I was really suffering. It was quite a business this walking lark, I can tell you. A real ordeal if you must know. And the heat – **WHEW!** It was like a glasshouse. A dry heat. A weight. It was all I could do to keep my lids open. I was ailing badly by the time our hostess arrived – but it was worth the wait.

This one was a real athlete. As big as a camel. She had muscles on her too, by the look of things. One could tell. Her thick neck powered out of her enormous red sweater just begging to be strangled. It supported a fine head packed with chiseled shapes. Her features were hard. A brute. Her hair was thick auburn and waved severely down to her broad shoulders. She was a real pleasure to look at. I couldn't take my eyes off her. I could hardly hold myself back. She had the kind of mouth I really like to punch.

'Hello, lads.' It was music. Deep, lusty, like a meathook.

'Who's your friend, Bradford? He looks a bit…yellow!'

'Oh, this is Viktor. He's a poet. You don't mind me bringing him along do you?'

'No. He's really rather handsome!'

She'd made my day!

I'd messed my kecks!

# The End

# DAGGER!

I lit a fag, sank a beer and crashed the bus into a dog. Then I burst through the door of a hut, ripping the gat from me mac.
'**DAGGER!**' I roared, running up the fucking stairs. '**DIRK DAGGER!**'

And that's when I saw **HER!**

She was fourteen and **BUILT!** My lung whistled as she inched stickily toward me.

Just then, me gat shit bullets everywhere! She stopped a gobful and popped.

Next, I see this other bloke and spring into action. I cut, hooked and kicked him. Hard. Pretty soon I was breaking arms, legs and ribs. Later, I snapped off fingers.

Anyway, back at the pub, I burst a pack of spots and poked a black in the pocket. Then, I cleaned up me lager and left.

Outside, I lit up a plug and sucked at it. Hot hard bullets of rain hit me mac. A baby cried. A pub shut. Another bus crashed... Thoughts flew through me head like footballs.

WHY had it all been so easy?

WHAT did the girl fit in?

WHERE was Deep Waterhouse, the fighting writer?

HOW would I kill him when I got him?

And WHEN would I get the fiver for doing it?

That's when it hit me. I needed an answer.

I needed four!

I gunned the heap over to Pug's Gym and shot out.

Loudly, I ran up the fucking stairs. '**STOP BOXING!!!**' I went, firing into a contender. 'Where's that **TWAT** Waterhouse!?!'

A seven-foot heavyweight bungled forward and went. 'He's punching his mate in the ring!'

Just then, Deep Waterhouse climbed through the ropes, gloves dripping. Instantly, I shot his foot, hip, ear and watch off but he got up and opened my face with his fists. I wanted his mates to pull him off but he didn't have any. He punched me outside. Then he punched me insides, too.

Then, unfortunately, a bloke burst in with two guns. **'STOP THAT, DAGGER!!!'** he roared. 'The contract's off! You squashed that copper's dog! **FLAT!**'

'What about the fiver?!' I flapped, surrealistically.

'Forget it, sucker! This is the punchline...'

**BANG!**

# The End

# WHEN I WAS YOUNG

Then, when I was with a sewage hire firm, it happened. I met Pat.

She was hot, dark, wet and tough. She had big tits, loads of money, a sports car and a lot of boxing trophies.

When we first met I was covered in shit. She had a figure-hugging pyrex dress with matching binoculars. Her bog was blocked. She wanted it plunged. Pierced. Sucked and cleaned. I did it. I played with it. I rubbed it on my bare flesh. I rolled it around in my mouth. I covered my entire body in it. **YEEEUCH!** I must have been mad!

## The End

# A TOWN CALLED EARLY

There wasn't much of anybody around as I moseyed up Main Street. The sound of lousy singing floated horrifically from the saloon as I parked my horse and went in.
    The first thing I saw was **HER!**
    Around the stage, two dozen drunken shitkickers were going crazy and not for her singing neither. The things she did with her hips were enough to make a man run out and

get himself a fat old cow to poke. The hair and breasts were longer but the voice could only belong to one woman. Betty-Lou Rolls.

'Sure could do with some jokes around here!' yelled an old timer, firing his guns in the air.

I was into my fifth finger when she finished her set. Then, she ran over and slipped her tits in my drink.

'If it ain't Hymn Witherspoon,' she panted, throbbily. 'Y'know you shouldn't come here.'

'Betty-Lou Rolls,' I said, fingering my red eye. 'It's been nine years. Nine long years... for **ME!**'

'They don't call me Betty no more, Hymn,' she shuddered noisily. 'I had to change my name after that thing you done to that pig. These days I'm known as Pussy le Tubes.'

'Pussy,' I said and, rolling my tongue around it, inserted two fingers in one swift movement. 'That's a mighty purty name.'

Just then she jerked me roughly. 'You shouldn't have come here, I tell you!' she gasped, pushing me out. 'If Big Red finds out you're here, he'll cut your head off, Hymn!'

'No Big Red Dobber scares me!' I roared, shooting off a load. 'That one-eyed snake! He's not that hard! I'll throttle him!'

'Can't you leave it alone?!' she shouted from behind her tits. 'It's been nine years since you two fell out. I know it's been hard, the way you've been banged up, Hymn. But he's Sheriff now. He'll kill you!'

'Let him try,' I sneered, bursting through the batflaps. 'I'll be waitin'!'

\* \* \* \* \*

    That night I couldn't sleep. I lay awake in my hotel room drinking, smoking and sweating. I was thinking about how to get hold of Red Dobber when my thoughts wobbled back. Back to when I had Pussy all to myself and Dobber and I were buddies. We stuck together through thick and thin. But then came that day. We'd robbed a payroll train near Fort Sierra when we got pinned down by a big posse. We were holed up till nightfall when Dobber plugged me from behind and, taking the money, left me for dead. But I didn't die. I was caught by the posse and banged up in a box for nine years. A day didn't go by in that stinking hole that I didn't think of that big Red Dobber nestling up to my Pussy. A day didn't go by when I wouldn't swear I'd have my revenge, my money and my woman. **BACK!**

    That morning, the sky was blood red and the birds were singing in the trees. Out on the street, a gaggle of young girls frolicked annoyingly as the townsfolk spilled out from the church in their Sunday best. I moved away from the window and quickly buffed my chaps. Then, admiring the length of my piece, I thrust it firmly into its sheath, strode manfully from the hotel and tightened my saddlebags.

'Hold it right there, Witherspoon,' growled a familiar voice from behind. 'You're under arrest!'

I whirled round to face the voice, my hand frozen above the butt of my gun. The frothing purple head before me told me everything: it was Sheriff Big Red Dobber himself, his 12-gauge levelled at the lapels of my double-breasted pants.

'I've come for my money, Red,' I sneered. 'And I aim to get it!'

'No-one carries a gun on Sundays,' Dobber went, blasting a hole in the air. 'Now drop 'em!'

I did it quick.

'I've got you just where I want you now,' he roared, blowing another hole in the air. 'I'm gonna break you. I'm gonna bust your ass so bad you're gonna crawl to me and beg to eat the saloon spittoon, Witherspoon.'

I knew right then that he'd blown off his full load, so I sprang up and launched a law-flooring poke to Dobber's brains. Quickly, the townsfolk rushed over and formed a cheering circle around us in which I punched, kicked, hung, bit and killed him. The crowd gasped as I clambered up onto the body and, tearing the star from his shirt, shit and pissed in his mouth.

Just then, Pussy ran over and brazenly flattened her front against my huge, blood-spattered chest. 'I've got the money!' she shrieked.

I looked hungrily at her soft, young blouse as it fought vainly to tame the two huge struggling orbs beneath it. I thought wildly about her hot pubic mound enveloping mine as her hips writhed against me. Her full, moist lips parted and a frantic tongue lashed out toward me as she smashed her mouth into mine. I threw her off brutally and backed away, wiping the blood from my lips. She crouched before me: an untameable, wild animal.

It's seeing Pussy spread out like that, I thought, that'd make any man come to Early.

## The End

# THINGY!

I'd handed the professor his pints and looked at the stars outside the pub. "Ere, Prof,' I'd romanticised, telepathically. 'I wonder what it's like in pubs on other planets.'

'Vell, kid,' he went, mentally. 'Dez only von vay to find out.' Quickly, we built a flying saucer and drove it to another world.

'**TAXI!**' I thought loudly, leaping down from the capsule.

Ssssss.

'Where to, earthlings?' forethought a triple-winged, four-headed eye in a blue suit. 'Pub tour?'

'After six months of all zat Lo-Grav brown study ve sure could use a drink!' the Prof laughed, climbing into the cab. We went through The Purple Valley into The Martian Landscape before we stopped at The J.G. Ballard Arms for a quickie. It was full of extremely glutinous, multi-winged putrescent things from every planet. Eighty thousand eyes followed us to the bar but I fought back the fear and ordered a round. My lager had a massive head on it.

'That'll be three hundred quid, pal!' it said.

'American Express?'

'Sorry, mate. We only take joke shop money in here. **BILLY!**'

Just then, a fruity, wet vapour oozed hideously from between my fiercely clenched buttocks as a massive, putrefying, blob-like mass with fists and Doc Martens ran up and kicked my head in.

'Professor! Quick! Get a gadget!'

Instantly, the Professor ripped out a brick and threw it. It hit the blob in the beak and stunned it. I leapt up and blew the head off my beer. 'You bastard!' it spat from the deck. 'You've burst our blob bouncer, Billy! Get them, lads!'

'**TAXI!**'

Sssssss.

'Where to now, earthlings?'

'Somewhere! **FAST!**'

Immediately, we got there. It was one of those yellow, neo-Tesco discos called The Sir Leslie Crowther. There was a huge bloated scaly thing on the door.

'Sorry, lads,' it went, adjusting the skin on its dicky. 'Martians only!'

'That's clever,' I laughed. 'Fancy having a Mars bar in Uranus!'

## The End

# THE MATCH!

**PHWEEEP!**
It began.
**KICK-OFF!**
**ROAR!!!**
What a ball!
**FOUL!**
**LOB!**
**PUNT!**
**TRAP!**
**GOOOOAAAALLLL!!!**
One-nil!
What a dribble!

**The End**

# JUNGLE BOY

So then I woke up in a jungle. I was three, hairy, and could swing from trees. When I was thirteen, I shagged my first chimp and was sick. See, I was a bloke!

One day, when I was larking about in the creepers, I swang into a hut and stopped. When I woke up I went in and found a book. Quickly, I learnt to read, write, and speak English, French, Belgian and Dutch. Suddenly, Dad swung up on a vine.

'What's all this, son?' he said, in Chimp. 'Don't fuck with books and that. You'll be building cities next and then we'll all be out of a job!'

'It's no good, Dad,' I replied, rolling a fag with my foot. 'I'm old enough to sign on! I'm off!'

In England none of the birds had hairs.
**GOOD!**

## The End

# NORTON BIKEMAN

## Chapter ONE

Through the fog Jet could hear the Doctor's muffled voice. '...a chance in a million ...lost all his blood ...irreparable internal damage ...skull in a thousand fragments ...we'd have to completely rebuild him from scrap!'

'You mean scratch, Doctor?'

'I'm telling you, I mean **SCRAP!!!**'

\* \* \* \* \*

Later, Jet was sitting up in bed buffing his headrest when a booster rushed in and yelled, 'Jet Norton, innit?!'

'Yeah!' Jet roared, fuming. 'What of it?!'

'The name's Deathtrap. Scooter Deathtrap, ace cub reporter for Leather Hog Monthly. Our readers want to know more about **YOU**! The first ever man to be totally rebuilt from bike bits!'

'Get to the point, bus filth!' Jet throttled noisily. 'I could kill a Castrol!'

'You'll get all the Castrol you want if you win the T.T. next week!'

Jet's cogs tightened. This was his big chance. He knew that if he won, he'd be the first ever 1000cc bloke to rule Bikeworld. His chrome forehead flashed triumphantly, his pistons pumped with horsepower, his leathers sprang to life.

'I'll do it!' he revved. 'I am **BIKEMAN!!!**'

However, shortly before the ferry, Jet was stolen and sold to an Artist who turned him into a toilet and everything went black...

# Chapter TWO

Through the fog Jet could hear the muffled wofflese of posh people. '...a bio-installation ...basic dialectical art movement ...it's got a log in it!' Then, suddenly, a familiar voice drifted through the haze.

   '**PSSST!** Bikeman! It's me! Deathtrap!'

   Jet woke like a rocket. '**WHERE AM I? WHAT AM I?**'

'You're a bog at the Wallasey Art Fair,' Scooter said, flatly. 'You've just been sold for twelve pound forty.'

Jet gulped, his ballcock sinking.

**'TAXI!!!'**

Later, Jet blubbed sloppily into his U-bend.

**'I'M A BOG! I'M A BOG!'** he sobbed, weakly. 'What colour am I?'

'Look, I know nowt about bikes,' Deathtrap confessed consolingly and, paying the cab, dragged Jet into a block of flats. 'But I know a bird who does!'

Twelve flights later they met Ute. 'Hi, boys,' she breathed, exposing the luscious pink expanse of her bedsit.

Jet flushed automatically.

She was six-foot four in her thigh-length, hip-hugging biker boots and high-impact nipple clips. He knew then and there that he loved her. This was **IT!**

That night, Ute stripped Jet down and began to fiddle with his banjo bolts and sludge traps as she lovingly rebuilt him. Eagerly, she reamed Jet's bush and got a nice sliding fit on his rod when, suddenly, Jet's sump leaked.

'Sorry, Jet,' Ute gasped, clocking his ball race. 'I didn't know you had a plug-oiling problem. Your block'll need boring.'

Jet turned over.

Carefully, Ute removed Jet's outer case and, liberally smearing his tensioner with grease, slowly moved his pistons with her bare hands. With that, Jet's nuts locked and he spurted onto the carpet.

**FLOB!**

Later, Jet nervously rubbed his ring with her rag.

'Er…will I still make the T.T., then?' he asked.

'Relax, Mr Norton,' Ute giggled playfully, tightening his nuts with a wrench. 'The way I've fettled you, you can win anything! You're part SS, part combat and commando! But you're all **BIKEMAN!**'

'**YES!**' thought Jet aloud as he studied himself in the mirror. '**NORTON BIKEMAN!**'

All of a sudden, Jet found himself on a racetrack, a colourful flag waving in the air.

**BANG!**
'They're off!'
**ZOOM!**
'The bikes go past!'
**ROAR!**
'The crowd go mad!'
**BOFF!**
'A bike blows up!'

'Yes, Murray, let's hope that this holiday crowd is in for the sort of spectacular two-wheeled, twin turbo frenzy the T.T.'s become so famous for!'

'**OH!** And here they come again, Barry!'

'Yes, Murray, at the start of the second it's **GEORGE MICHAELJACKSONACMEFRITHHANHANHARDLY WALKATALL**, and the late entry spurting into the rear, **BIKEMAN!**'

'Yes, Barry, that's Norton Bikeman, the man at the centre of all the controversy! Half-man, half-bike, he's the first ever bloke to be totally rebuilt from bike bits! I was reading in The Sun this morning that it's his ambition to become the first ever 1000cc bloke to rule Bikeworld!'

'Well, Murray, with four laps to go, I don't think this young metal lad from Wallasey, handicapped by his dodgy starter dog, can match the wily talents of these grizzled veterans!'

'**OH!** And Bikeman roars into the lead as they start the fourth!'

'**HA-HAH!**' Jet laughed, biking brilliantly. 'I'm going to **WIN!**' And with that he burst by Braddan, streaked through Baaregarroo, vroomed along the Verandah and whipped round Windy to the Grandstand twice when, suddenly, Jet's recess blocked uncomfortably.

'**OOOF!**' he thought, leaking openly. 'I need a pit-stop!'

Seconds later, Ute was giggling and grabbing lovingly at his sludge trap plugs, but Jet wasn't happy.

'It's your flange!' he snapped. 'It's too tight! Can't you lubricate it a lot?!'

Hours seemed to pass as Ute fiddled frantically with his recess, bush and bevel sump, smeared a suspect rod liberally with WD40 and, plating his gusset, burst into tears. 'It's no good, Jet, you can't finish! You're a deathtrap!'

'Never mind,' Scooter purred annoyingly. 'You can win other races.'

Instantly, Jet drove back onto the track and accelerated noisily amidst a thick plume of black smoke. '**HA!**' he went, cerebrally. '**BOLLOCKS!**'

'Well, Murray, that's a comprehensive reaming the metal lad's had from his buxom German mechanic but he's back in seventeenth place and now, barring any terrific last lap dramatics, there's absolutely no way he can win!'

'OH! He's done it! **NORTON BIKEMAN WINS BY A HEAD! HIS HEAD!**'

'**I'VE WON!**' Jet spluttered weakly and, waving his cup aloft, scanned the crowd for Ute. 'I've **WON!**'

But Ute was gone...

## Chapter THREE

Jet Norton was a star! And he knew it! The first ever Bikeman to win the TT, by morning his face would be known throughout the planet. From the sizzling, sun-kissed beaches of the Bahamas and the celebrity-packed world of palaces and parties, to the seedy, vice-ridden discos of Europe, scantily clad, Bounty-gobbling babes would drool over his big end, his recess and plugs. Girls that wouldn't have looked at him twice as a mere old fashioned biped would now fight for photos of his fuel cock and ball-race.

But the last lap had virtually killed Jet and, as he spluttered weakly into the winner's enclosure, he knew that his dream would have to wait. No, there'd be no after-race victory shag tonight. No one to squirm damply beneath him or to arch and writhe playfully so that he could notice the Alpine magnificence of their breasts as they loomed hugely in the bedroom. Instead, Jet collapsed and woke up three days later back in Britain, his frame racked with pain and his wheels gone!

'Welcome to the land of the living, Norton,' hissed a voice from the shadows of his rigid rear end. 'But not for long! **HA-HAH!**'

'What are you doing, Scooter?' revved Jet, vibrating his ring aggressively. 'Is this a joke? Why am I half-stripped and wheel-less?!'

Quickly, the ace cub reporter for Leather Hog Monthly explained the plot and, leaving Jet's life dripping away through a dodgy valve, shot off with the winnings.

Days later, while Jet angrily turned over in the dole, he had plenty of time to think about the heroic, physically impossible way in which he'd saved himself. Then, suddenly, Jet's number came up and, screeching up to the counter, he roared, 'The name's Norton! Jet Norton! First ever Bikeman to win a T.T. race…'

'I'm afraid there don't appear to be any vacancies for motorbikes at the moment,' said the O level-less blob in the bulletproof booth. 'So we'll put you down for the… **JOB CLUB!**'

Jet's O-ring dug painfully into his nuts and a little drop of oil plopped to the lino when he heard a familiar voice…

## Chapter FOUR

'I didn't save you from one of those M25 pile-ups just so you could claim Job Seeker's Allowance!' Jet's rod throbbed excitedly, his gadgets agog, as the familiar, silver-lipped brogue brought back a flood of hazy memories. It was Olaf! Doktor Olaf Petersen, PhD, DNA & BSA, whose lone dedication to Organic Mechanics had, just two chapters ago, saved Jet from the Big Sleep in the Wooden Kimono. 'Jet!' he cried. **'YOUR COUNTRY NEEDS YOU! TAXI!!'**

Later, in the Lab, Jet parked in the corner, snug and safe, as the surgeon sterilised his stuff. As Jet watched, everything seemed like a distant nightmare, a bad dream from which he was waking. The world considered him a freak, the Doktor a butcher, but the truth was that Olaf towered magnificently above a medical world that heaped scorn upon him for his unorthodox and experimental practices. Practices that some considered nothing more than bungled atrocities! Yet Petersen had licked the greatest brains mankind could throw at him and tasted victory, successfully entering a V8 bloke in the Arsenal FC Stockcar Cup in 1961. Now, thirty years later, minds boggled at his latest prototype: half-man, half-bike. Jet Norton was the world's only living machine.

Wiping his seat vigorously with a damp rag, the eminent disemboweller allowed himself a jocular but sinister smirk. 'They may have laughed at us, Jet,' said the surgeon, a storm brewing outside. 'By the time I've finished, they'll never dare laugh again!'

Then, before Jet could blurt out the catalogue of catastrophes that had befallen him, from his Castrol addiction to his psychotic fear of skidmarks, the great Doktor straddled him and, ripping open his sump, plunged in a dipstick of terrifying proportions.

'**OUCH!**' yelped Jet, his starter dog biting into two overworked nuts. 'That hurts!'

'What's a little pain compared to the miracle I am about to perform?!' chuckled Olaf, lighting a blowtorch with his fag.

'For years, those Stone Age, syringe-jabbing, belly-burgling quacks laughed openly at my experiments. They said it could never be done! That the union of flesh and metal was an impossible dream!'

With that, the legendary Dok gelled a rubber cap and forced it noisily into Jet's gaping hole.

Jet winced.

'Yet I have proved them wrong! Proved the world wrong! By the time I'm finished, that very same world will quake with fear! **HA-HAH!**'

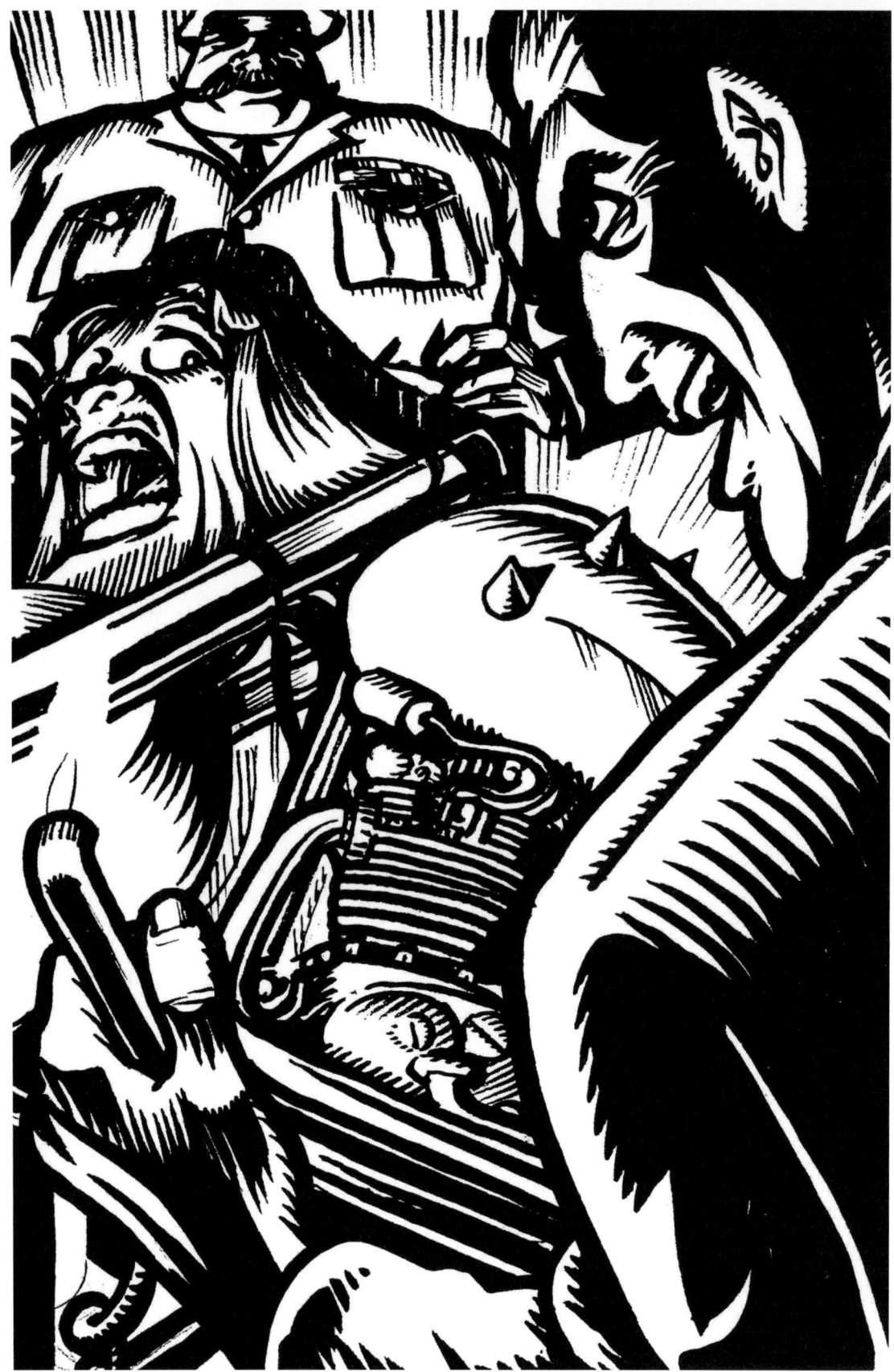

Jet gulped when the door burst open and a phalange of over-decorated army bigwigs erupted into the Lab, led by the infamous Major P.V.C. 'Bomber' Jacket whose eager young privates sweated under the weight of a huge box. Seconds later, as several shiny, red-ended rockets and a variety of other projectiles were lifted from the crates, Jet's ring dropped, cracking his nuts.

'Well, Dok!' the Bomber barked, doing something. 'What's the M.O.?!'

'Operation Shit-She-ite right on schedule,' smiled Olaf, fingering Jet. 'By 1800 hours, Private Jet here will be all yours. This new crankcase will give you provision for a front-mounted laser sight and a rear flange-fitting grenade launcher. Automatic ignition via **HUD** allowing the rocker oil drain pipes to be scrapped and replaced by twin six-barrelled .50 mil cannons and, of course, telescopic forks to accommodate the weight of the new mini-sidewinders.'

'That's easy for you to say, Dok,' Jet yelled in alarm. 'But what does it all mean for me…?!'

'It means, Private Jet,' smirked Bomber cruelly, twisting his handlebars, 'that by 0600 hours tomorrow, you'll be dropped and deployed operationally somewhere in the Middle East where you'll be issued your Top Secret, Eyes-Only orders. Now…get your fucking hair cut!!!'

That night, sellotaped beneath the screaming fuselage of the F117 as it flew invisibly over the Med, Jet began to think…**TWICE!**

*TO BE CONTINUED…*

Editor's note: These stories were originally commissioned by Bike magazine in the late 80s. However, the magazine went bust shortly after the second issue was published and the saga was never completed.

# OFF-DUTY

**IT** was one of those balmy summer days that blows cool in the evenings as I sat in the car park of the pub, sipping a lager and feeling the sweat grow cold beneath my shirt. We were off-duty and loving every minute of it. It was a relief to change out of the hot serge trousers and nylon shirt and sit outside with a beer.

The girls, their brown legs scissoring seductively, swayed past in a cloud of perfume and giggles. They eyed us. We eyed them back. We were big lads and they knew it. They went inside. I leant back against the fender of a car and breathed in the summer air.

It beat working.

I'd had a gutful of police work. It was a messy, dirty, sick-making grind. But it was a job.

## The End

# GRAILWOOD

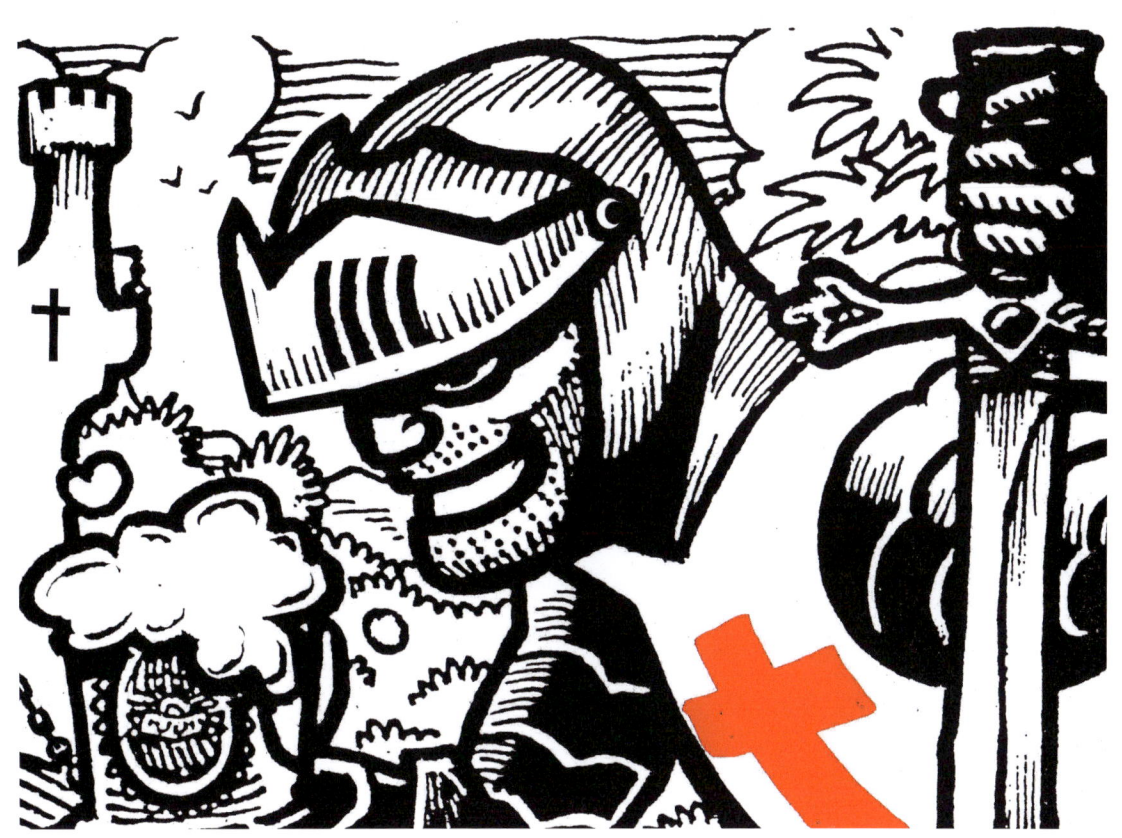

**Our story begins long ago, in the Northland, where be Grailwood. Legend has it that every man had his own pub and women cooked daily.**

## The End

# ¡TOROS!

The name's Adore. Matt Adore. Bullfighter, si. One day, I was stabbing a bull in the ring when, high up in the stand, I saw **HER!** It was Conchita dos Gallons, the famous Flamenco dancer.

Just then, I felt a hard horn in my pantitos and, pulling a face, saw a bullock shoot off. The crowd gasped. I saw the look of horror on her face, her eyes and breasts close together in the distance. Quickly, I whirled round to face the bull.

It was two tons of homicidal beef with a frothing purple head. It clawed the ground with four enormous hoofs and laughed. Suddenly, without warning, it charged toward me.

When I woke up I had a feed. A drip feed. Later, a doctor roamed up and went, 'You're a very lucky man, Senor Adore. Your wounds are well on their way to recovery. You will have noticed that your ring is missing but don't worry. We have put this in an envelope with your privates. By the way, you have a visitor. A very famous Flamenco dancer.'

'¿¡Conchita dos Gallons?!'

'Correct,' she breathed near me. '¿Fancy a grape?'

She was everything I'd ever wanted and more. I could smell the sensuous, languid perfume on her big breasts. I heard the soft, fleshy mounds of my buttocks grip the sheet. I saw her do something subtly sensual and felt myself come toward her.

'¡Conchita!' I gushed in my pyjama pantitos. '¡¿Is it really you?!'

'In the flesh,' she purred. '¡¿SI?!'

'¡I love you!' I screamed dramatically. '¡Say the word and I would do anything for you!'

'Come quickly, then get dressed and follow me.'

Later, in a booth at the Santa de Lager Hotel, she told me her plan. It was easy. We were to put all our savings on the bull in the next fight and I was to take a dive. I said I'd do it and did. But I got caught by the bullocks and died.

# The End

# THE GLADIATORS!

Two thousand years ago, Tony Antonionionioni was working with a Libyan rock group. He'd been a slave since birth and he'd grown up to hate the sight of rocks with a vengeance that would one day make his name legend...

What happened was Tony was chewing on a Roman hamstring sandwich when, suddenly, Peter Insidovus rode up scouting talent for his new act, The Gladiators.

'Fancy a job, lad?' he roared in Latin. 'Can you handle a sword?'

'Only a pork sword,' Tony gritted uncomfortably, spitting out a heel. 'What's the pay?'

'Wine, women and combat. Plus, little boys and chickens.'

'Sounds good,' went Tony, packing his away kit. '**I'LL DO IT!**'

Five years later, Tony had battled his way to the peak of gladiatorial perfection. He'd been socked, slugged, coshed and clubbed into shape by many hours of brutal training and discipline. But he loved it. Anything was better than rocks.

One day, Peter Insidovus burst into the barracks with bad news. 'Look, lads, it's like this. This famous Roman Consul, Publicus Publicanus, wants to see two of you fight to the death. Volunteers step forward...'

The men shifted unnaturally in their sandals as the sound of tittering women floated in through the sunlit window. A dog barked. A young bird flew in... then flew out again.

'Right then, you two! Tony! Woody! Come here!'

Tony gaped at his mate in horror. 'He wouldn't make us fight to the death would he, Woody?'

'Not if I kill you first, honky!'

'That's the spirit, Woody,' went Peter Insidovus, rubbing his hands vigorously. 'Now, you and Tony slip into your skimpy gladiator gear and I'll meet you on the pitch in five minutes. Kick-off's at two-thirty.'

'Fvck you!' Tony wailed, splashing about in his puddle.

'When I signed up, you said we'd have wine, women, little boys and chickens, Insidovus! You lied! The lads and me are fed up. Or should be. I mean, why should I stab my mate in the ring publicly?'

'It's either that or back to the slabs for you, Rocky!'

'No one calls me Rocky and lives!' raged Tony, knocking Insidovus out, thus igniting a revolution that swept across the Roman Empire.

However, many expensive bloodbaths later, Tony and his men were caught by the Cohorts of Publicus Publicanus. 'Which one of you is Tony the Gladiator?'

'We all are!' roared the slaves.

'Fair enough,' said Publicanus. 'Hang the lot!'

# The End

# PARA!

It's good fun being a para, see. We get to go to hot places where we kill people in lots of weird and wonderful ways. Take last week. Me and the lads were punching each other in the arsenal when Colonel R.G. Basher burst in. '**HUT!**' he yelled, generally. 'Report to the mess immediately for orders! Last orders!'

Quickly, we raced over and were drinking them when General P.V.C. 'Bomber' Jacket crashed in with the lad with the small arms. '**AHOY!**' he went, unnaturally. 'What you lads need is a war! Any war! And I know just the man to start it. **ME!**'

Instantly, we leapt into a plane and flew off. Later, when we were high up, we jumped out and landed. **SNAP!!! HA-HAH!** You don't need parachutes when you're as tough as us!

Anyway, up ahead we could make out a small village nestling peacefully in a lush valley full of timid, four-legged thingies that we shot and ate.

'Where are we?' I whispered, privately.

'Who cares, kid?!' 'Bomber' hollered. '**CHARGE!**'

Later, after several minor bloodbaths, we piled into the pub and shot everyone but the barman, as usual. See, we like to nail their tongues to the floor and kick 'em around the room. That way they don't complain while we're raping their beer.

## OFFICIAL!!!

# THE SEA!

The sea! The sea!
The beautiful, untameable wild! The cut of wind. The squall of rain. The fury of the waves. The fist of storm cut loose to punch the very planet! The sea! The sea! Its might! Its sheer, abundant power! The giver and taker of life!

## The End

# DING!

Nobby's life was shit. He gazed gloomily through the greasy grille at the grey, grimy grids of Glumly's grubby backstreets and farted miserably. It seemed like only yesterday when he'd been at the peak of physical perfection and a contender for heavyweight boxing's greatest honour: **MONEY!**

But, suddenly, his career took a dive when he was cruelly disqualified after doctors found a small, illegal brain in Nobby's locker. He was left a broken, lonely fat man.

Just then, Nobby's ex-manager and father figure, Sturgeon Merrydown, burst in with the Evening Liar. 'Look Nobby!' he screamed horrifically, waving it in the air. 'It's your big chance for a comeback! The world champion, Apollo Moonshot, has challenged any man in the world to beat him! Whaddaya say?!'

'Durrrrrh!' yelled Nobby, excitedly.

During the following weeks Nobby sparred, skipped, jogged and sweated his way into the Evening Liar headlines. He was a hero. Apollo Spaceship watched horrified as Nobby punched a pig in the belly on telly.

Eventually, the night of the big fight came round. He was nervous. He was shitting bricks. Sturgeon picked one up and slipped it into his glove.

'Go get him Nobby!'

**DING-DING!**

Fifteen rounds later, Nobby had been battered into a multi-coloured blob-like mess of bone and jelly. Heroically, he struggled to his knees and launched a blistering onslaught but took a clout to the throat and crumpled. As the sound of the count echoed in his ears, images of the grim, grimy slums

of Glumly flashed through Nobby's head. Suddenly, he was back on his feet in the middle of the fray but there was nowhere to hide from Apollo Landing's ferocious textbook attack: punch, left, right, straight left, uppercut, jab, hook and haymaker.

**OOOOF! OOOF! OOOF! OOOF! OOOF! OOOF! OOOF! OOOF! KNOCKOUT!**

Two months and four operations later, Nobby came to in a swank Hollywood beach house with Sturgeon at his side. He wondered where he was. 'Don't worry, Nobby,' smiled Sturgeon, handing him a Porsche. 'I put everything we own on Apollo Splashdown to win and bought all this with the winnings!'

'**DURRRRH!**' roared Nobby ecstatically. '**FUCKIN' DURRRRH!**'

# The End

# WHEN WOMEN COME TO PUBS

Nothing ever really happened in the Pub until one of the regulars suddenly brought in a woman. It was the biggest event the locals could remember and people came from all over the area to pack into the Pub for a look. After all, this was a thing a man might never live to see again. This was a woman! In a Pub! And she was all woman alright. She was all woman and more.

Neil was upset. He'd brought his girlfriend into the Pub to have a good time with her. But now the place was thick with blokes all trying to get her attention. They were dancing about like excited puppies and punching each other for fun. Sure, Neil had known some other girls but none like her. She was a real woman and he'd do anything to keep her.

He nursed his Pint at the Bar while the crowds pushed and shoved boisterously about his bird. 'You won't be able to keep this one, Neil!' one of them yelled. 'Men aren't supposed to have a woman all the time!'

'Well, I want one all the time,' Neil said, pushing them back. 'I'm fed up of waiting all week just to grab a granny at the weekend.'

Everybody whooped and hollered. 'You're off your heid!' they laughed.

All the girls in Waterloo knew Neil wanted a girl all the time but Neil never did anything about it. Except on a Friday or a Saturday night. Then he'd drown a few pints and sweet-talk all the girls and tell them everything they'd always wanted to hear. But come Sunday, Neil would always be gone.

The local girls weren't classy enough for him. He wanted a woman. A real woman. With ways. Special ways. He'd seen their pictures in magazines and now he wanted one of his own all the time. He didn't want to have to wait till the weekends anymore and play with the local girls. He wanted the sort he'd seen in glossy magazines. And now he had one.

She had tight clothes and stay-up stockings and it was plain to everyone that she was an absolute babe. She had the sort of ways some men had never seen before. They thumped each other excitedly around her. But she was Neil's girl now and he was bursting to tell everyone just what they were missing.

He was telling anyone who'd listen about how much skimpy underwear she had and what sort of stuff she could do with them lips. And right there is when he made the biggest mistake of his life.

The Pub erupted. Blokes were keen to kill to get a look at some of those things Neil was talking about. There was punching and kicking and biting and gouging and furniture was being smashed all over the place. The blokes were having the time of their lives fighting to get a peek at Neil's girl.

They kept on fighting until the Pub closed and Neil's girl left, and then they began to drift home. They were keen to get back and tell everyone about the night a woman came into the Pub.

## The End

# ME, MANIAC!

## Chapter ONE

I ploughed into the heap and drove it. When I got fed up, I crashed into a kid and got out. It was Jimmy's Gym & Deli, where arseholes were locked for combat and pugilists punched, poked, and pasted people publicly.

In the Ring!

But their type don't scare me. No one scares me. Not even a Cubist.

Nah. When it comes to murder and the slaughter of the innocent, I'm your man.

Just then, a boxer burst in with a Beretta and, levelling it at my head, pulled focus and shot me. I went down, spilling my pint.

## Chapter TWO

Several days and two racy sequels later, I came to splashing about in a pool of blood and lager. There was a big crowd and a couple a cops posing for tourist shots. I knew then that if the eyes of the mob had mouths they'd be as thirsty as hell to see that blood.

Murder should be a spectator sport.

## Chapter THREE

When I woke up I was running. I didn't know why I was running. I just was. When I looked over my shoulder I saw four blokes. They were running too. Then it hit me. They were running after me. They were cops!

Quickly, I ran out of a door, down some steps, across a road, through an entry, over a wall and into a street with an end. A dead end. So, I stopped, shot one, stabbed one, broke a bunch of legs and ran off. See, it didn't bother me none. In my profession we get sapped, slugged, shot and tortured but a couple of pints later and we're right back at it. Night or day. Rain or shine. Suddenly, I tripped on me shoelace and got caught.

The Feds were standing over me. Them and their guns. They were looking at me with their mouths open… gulp…

…so were the cops.

# The End

# CUB-COP!

It's a good laugh being a police dog, see. Take last week. Slobbering, I burst into this room, the lads in blue behind me. I barked. Instantly, these three punks left this big bag of coke and bolted. I leapt in and got a fucking good snort before the cops kicked me off. But it was worth it!

**The End**

# DYKE!

Boyishly, I slipped into a fresh donkey jacket and thundered down to The Limp Dick and Dung Puncher. It was jammed with birds when I got there. Quickly, I stole a pint, propped me bulk against the bar and eyed up the talent.

It was worth watching.

I was surrounded by hot, moist mobs of teenage lovelies, their bodies crushed against me. Just then, I noticed a pert young horsewoman in a pair of slit-splitting Levi's as she inched stickily through the writhing mass toward me.

'**OI!**' I roared, grabbing her subtly by the tits. 'Show us yer piss-flaps!'

'You brute!' she squealed timidly. 'Let's go. **TAXI!**'

In the cab she told me how she was a struggling actress.

In the Spud Hut, she told me how her dad had when she was young and later, back at her place, how she'd been by her teacher as well.

'Shut it and get naked!' I snarled, breaking me coffee.

At first she fought like a wildcat, scratching and biting, but I like that. So then I pinned her to the rug and she liked that. Her thick wet lips parted to reveal thick wet teeth. They bit me.

Manfully, I tore aside the flimsy folds of her blouse and, unlacing me monkey boots, strapped a leather dick to me. She gasped at the size of it and arched upwards, exposing the luscious pink interior of her handbag.

I could smell the saddle leather on her hair, the straw on her jeans and the manure on her breath. Her body writhed around beneath me. I looked at it and lunged. She yelped and squirmed, bucked and writhed, heaved and panted as it went in and out again continuously.

Eventually, we both came noisily and squatted a house in Lambeth.

## The End

# I, THE BREWERY

It began with a dame and ended with a bang. But that's another story.

This one started when someone kidnapped, tortured, raped and strangled my family. **ME!** Suddenly, the phone rang savagely. I wrenched it brutally from the bloodstained cradle and smashed it to my teeth. **'HELLO!'** I roared fiercely, ripping the head off a Hundred Pipers and jamming it in. **'WHAT?!'**

'It's da Fizzy Lambrusco job, Mike.' It was my buddy, Pot. Detective Pot Chambers, the cleanest dick this side of the Big Drink. Ever since he'd blocked that chainsaw meant for me, I'd do anything for Pot. 'Forensics have matched da slug we ripped out of him with da one dat plugged Hymie Kangaroo-Downesport and Bugsy Bunnioni. And dat's not all dey have in common either, Mike. It turns out dat dey're both Cops!'

'Cop killer, huh?'

'Dat's right, Mike. Find him, and shoot him!'

I slammed down the blower in a steaming blue funk. Then, I changed into a red one and went out. My guns were straining eagerly in my jeans. I took them out and fired them. I was sure to find the killer this way. I was wrong. Reloading, I got to thinking. Then drinking. When I think I drink. That's me all over. Alky. Alky Pone. But my mates call me Mike.

Anyway, after a long and complicated 144-page paperback in which I polished off several Hundred Pipers, Pot got smoked and the dame got stabbed in the Crutchley Arms Motel, I found the killer holed up in a brothel on the last page. I shot him straight off. Hard. In the head. Twice. Loudly. As he died he blurted out the real killer's name...it was **ME**!

As usual! That's what happens when I drink. Y'see, in a world trembling in fear at the threat of death by nuclear war, toxic pollution and AIDS, the greatest threat of all is bullets!
**MINE!**

## The End

# OUTBACK!

Bruce Abodingo was wrenching a beer from the fridge when, suddenly, a naked sheila darted past. He leapt from the porch and sprang after her. She ran as fast as she could, but he was faster.

Roughly, Bruce grabbed her and wrestled her to the ground. She struggled passionately beneath him, kicking up big clouds of hot dust. He was snorting and straining. She was wild, wet, and scratched.

They were both sweating. **'STREWTH!'** he burst. 'A damp patch! Well, I'll be a koala in a cod piece! A beaver in the outback!'

'I was just looking for a kiwi in the bush,' she panted.
She got one.

## The End

# THE WEDDING

**GUNTER** waited. Another five minutes didn't seem to matter. He'd already waited twenty-three years. A few more minutes couldn't hurt. No, nothing could hurt now. Not now she was his. After all these years.

More than once he'd been tempted to give up hope. But Gunter had always known that he could never stop loving her. All his life, every beat of his heart had been hers. Yes, he loved her. He had always loved her. He loved her because she was **MAD!**

Yes, Pat was no ordinary woman. She was untameable. Wild. She ate with her hands. Drank like a man. Joked with the troops. She was a woman. Every inch a lady. A classy moll. Men had died for her. They still did. But now Pat O'Hagg had turned herself over to him. Gunter Larson. She was ready to raise pigs and bring up a family. All she wanted now was his love.

But in these last few minutes Gunter had thoughts he didn't want. Perhaps Pat would be jealous of his love for the land. Could she learn to love the soil? The taste of it? The smell of it? Perhaps she would grow bored and run off to the city. But then Gunter smiled. He knew she'd love the soil. He knew because she was **MAD!**

# DR. O!

I woke up with a massive throbbing purple head on me. Looking down, I saw an expensive laser beam inching toward my dick. I tried to get up but I was strapped uncomfortably to a steel thingy. Just then the notorious Dr. Olaf Peterson stepped forward from the gloom, a crushed puppy in each of his metal hands. 'Hello, James, old boy,' he croaked through his metal throat in English. 'In precisely three minutes your cock will resemble a smoked kipper. **HA-HAAH!**'
I felt the hot beam on my jeans as my testicles scuttled sideways to safety. I wrenched at my bonds frantically but it was no good – I was fucked. '**WAIT!**' I blurted. 'I'll talk!'

'Too late, James,' the Doktor cackled, hitting another fluffy puppy with a metal stick. 'Your little secrets don't interest me. I do this for fun. **HA-HAH!**'

'Not so fast, Peterson. You've forgotten one thing. My memoirs! They're locked securely in a safe-deposit box in a top people's bank in Knightsbridge!'

'Too late again, James. In sixty seconds precisely a massive metal Filofax, which at this moment is suspended from a satellite high above the earth, will drop onto London's West End and completely flatten the entire working population of England! **HA-HAH!**'

Surprisingly, I escaped and, after a lot of well-choreographed fighting in expensive subterranean locations, there was a series of huge explosions and I came to on a glamorous woman in the middle of the Pacific Ocean. I ripped out my special secret agent condom and put it on but, suddenly, it changed into an ex-US Navy aircraft carrier and brasserie which took us back to England just in time to save London and collect my knighthood. Again.

## The End

# SHERWOOD

Once upon a pint there were three brothers: **ROCKWOOD**, **THUD** and **ELVIS THUG** and they lived in a wood. Sherwood, to be precise.

One day, they were all dieting in the wood when they saw a triar. Triar Fuck. He was just about to tuck into a substantial green picnic basket when the **THUG** Bros. swung over and landed.

'**GRUB?**' they went. '**FUCK!**' Instantly, the triar got up and fled, leaving his dirk unsheathed behind him.

'**GROUSE!**' **ROCKWOOD** roared merrily. 'Innit?!'

Greedily, the **THUG** Bros. consumed the entire contents leaving a little pile of nowt.

'I'm gutted!' burped **THUD THUG**, wiping his lip with a squirrel. '**YEAH!**' sang **ELVIS**, strumming his lute. 'I could murder a mead meself!'

And so, with that, they set off. Later, in The Sheriff of Nottingham, **THUD THUG** rushed up to the bar and stopped. '**WENCH!**' he boomed. 'Twelve pints of the Merry Green Mead!'

Just then, olde Bob Hood wheezed up and went. 'Any chance of a pinte for ye olde mate, lads?'

'None,' sneered **ELVIS** in the obviously reptilian haircut that made the local archers quiver. 'So fuck off!'

Meanwhile, **ROCKWOOD THUG** was going mad with his arrows when a big bloke burst in with the Holy Grail.

'**YOINKS!**' went **THUD THUG**. 'Giz it!'

Brutally, he snatched it from the bloke and unscrolled it to the sports page where he saw a large ad:

'Oi! **ELVIS**,' roared **THUD**. 'Cop a load of this!'

**ELVIS** slid up and looked. '**WIFE…?! YAK!!!**' he snorted, expertly. 'Fuck that!'

Stunned, olde Bob Hood looked up at **ELVIS** in shock.

'Surely thou jest, lad? Canst thou not already taste the lake of lager mentioned above?'

'Lager Lake?!' went **ELVIS**. 'I'll do it!' And with that the **THUG** Bros. stormed from the pub, a horde of cheering locals hot on their heels behind them.

'Sir Baz de Rathbone,' blurted a bloke blowing a bugle. 'One hundred and eighty!'

Just then, **ROCKWOOD, THUD** and **ELVIS THUG** burst out from nowhere, accompanied by their now famous intrepid stench. The crowd gasped as **ROCKWOOD** ran up. Meanwhile, **THUD THUG** grabbed the bloke by the bugle and broke it. 'Ay up, you idle spermbank,' he growled. 'Our kid **ELVIS** wants a go!'

'I'm sorry sir but your reptilian brethren is too late,' went the bloke, dying.

'Go 'ead, **ELVIS**!' laughed **THUD**. 'You're on!'
'**YEAH!**' screamed **ROCKWOOD** from above. 'Where's me tights!?'

Casually, **ELVIS** fired off three quick shots.
**THUNK! THUNK! THUNK!**
And won.
And all were drunk in Sherwood.

## **OFFICIAL!!!**

# FAG!

Just then a plump prefect burst into the staffroom. 'Sir!... Sir!... Come quickly!' he squealed in upper class.

'How dare you use a staff entrance without permission, Porkins!' spluttered an erect member of staff. 'Have you no respect, boy?! This school has a great tradition to uphold! We've educated some of the finest homosexual defectors ever to disgrace the leather bars of Moscow!'

With that, an ageing maths master trundled forward unpleasantly and poked the prefect in the eyes. 'It's young, toffee-arsed scum like you what gives this school a bad name!' he hissed bitterly with his lips.

'B...but Sir...!' yelped Porkins, in pain.

'I don't know what this school's coming to,' grumbled the history teacher as he lay smoking by the fire. 'Only last week I caught two naked boys strung up by the cloisters.'

'That's nothing,' chuckled a jovial fat fellow. 'When I woke up this morning there was a frightened fourth former beneath me. Quickly, I penalised him for being out of school uniform, and made him give me six of the best...'

'B...but Sir!' blurted Porkins. 'Sir!'

'Oh for heaven's sake,' groaned the staff. 'What on earth is it, boy?'

'Sir! Wupert Everwett's being bummed alive in the bogs, Sir!'

'He can be bummed flat as far as I'm concerned,' spluttered an enraged purple Head. 'As long as he doesn't miss his period!'

## The End

# NUTTER!

Back in the summer of '58, I was just another fat American teenager with spots. One day, I was on my way home from school when I banged into Jamie-Lee Clitoris on my skateboard.

'**OOOOF!**' she gasped, dropping her box and that in a puddle. 'Aw gee, Tommy, now you've gone and got my Lit all wet!'

Suddenly, the soundtrack changed from rock to eerie electronic music when Dr. Duck Pheasant slid up. 'You'd better get off the streets, kids,' he hissed in an unconvincing American accent. 'There's a chainsaw loony on the loose!'

'Oh no!' I yelped, quivering in my Harrington. 'My mom and pop are away for the weekend! What'll I do?!'

Just then it got dark quick. 'Don't worry, Tommy,' Jamie squirmed, tucking her Lit back into her folders.

'So are mine. Why don't you stay with me? I've got huge portions of Mickey Mouse Jell-O burgers and Jumbo fries over easy on rye. With chocolate mayo!'

Hours later, we were curled up watching 'Blind the Wife' with our T.V. snacks when there was a loud crash and, suddenly, there was a huge loony in the room.

Bbbbzzzzzzzzzzzzzz. Bzzz. Bzzz. Bbzzzzzzz. **MISSED!**

Bzzz. Bzzz. Bzzz. **MISSED!**

Bzzz. Bzzz. Bbzzzzzzz. Bzzzphkcuzhrtczpfugggh!

'**AAAAARRGH!!!**' He got me! Then he turned on Jamie.

'Hiya, kids!' he overacted badly. 'I'm a crazed alien / zombie / leper / pirate / vampire on acid! I've come to take my revenge on the thousand maniacs who torched me to death in my Dad's Chicken Giblet Hut on Halloween Friday that day on Elm Street 8 in 3-D!'

Suddenly, there was a major continuity error as Jamie and I ran to the upstairs of the bungalow to escape. The huge loony followed us despite the fact that we'd stabbed, kicked, punched, impaled, hung, guillotined, strangled, choked, smothered, drowned, shot and killed the cunt. However, after a lot of screaming and loud, intense music, Dr. Duck Pheasant erupted into the room and threw the huge loony out of the fourth floor window.

When he hit the ground it split open and thousands of well-paid biblical extras fell screaming into the huge chasm. Meanwhile, well-lit spaceships clashed overhead resulting in an expensive intergalactic nuclear holocaust when, suddenly, three hundred lawyers crashed onto the set.

'**CUT!!!**' they screamed, legally. 'This story is thirty million over budget!'

# The End

# SUMO!

## OOOF!!!

### The End

# TOP!

The name's Tebbit. Joseph Tebbit. Poor people call me 'Sir'. They have to. That's because I'm rich. Not posh though 'cos I was poor once, too. But that was years ago back in Slum-under-Belly, near Pubford.

I remember the day I started my first job. Mum bustled about all flustered. 'There you go, Joe,' she cooed, proudly. 'You do look nice in your dad's old suit.'

'But Mum,' I moaned, packing a box with butties. 'I don't want to be an undertaker at the mill! I want to be a **BOSS!**'

'Now don't you go getting ideas above your station, my lad!' Mum scolded, fingering her Hotpoint. 'Your dad's been an undertaker at the mill for years. Now behave yourself and bugger off.'

So off I trudged up the lonely wet cobblestones toward the lonely wet mill when, suddenly, a fat bobby crashed into me on his bike. 'Ay up, young 'un,' he laughed cheerfully. 'Not to worry. You look like you'll be the Boss of that lonely wet mill one day!'

Six months later, after a lot of grovelling, greasing, grassing and golf, I met the Boss' daughter at the Pubford Club. She helped me find my ball in the rough.

'You're not posh!' she breathed hungrily. 'Are you?'

'So what?' I snarled tensely, glaring at her properly for the first time. I looked at her feet and hands. I looked at her arms and hair. But I didn't dare look at her breasts.

'You'll never get it in the hole from there, Joe,' she giggled. 'Why don't you just putt it in?'

I did.

Later, when we were married, the Boss made me big in the business I inherited when he died accidentally on a fire. Quickly, I built a vast global conglomerate based on the bestselling books by Harold Robbins and died doing it.

# HOOLIGAN!

'**MUM!**' Joe screamed, stabbing a fish. 'I want me **MUM!**'

Schoolgirl Sally giggled and perched naughtily on the settee. 'Joe,' she moaned realistically. 'I need a **FUCK!**'

'Tough! I'm goin' the **PUB!**'

The Pub 'n Club was packed with hooligans in scarves.

'Wotcha, Joe,' went Box, punching a barman. 'Wotcha drinking?'

'**YOURS!**' he roared, lifting his lager and laughing. Box blew up. 'Wotcha doin'?' he shouted. 'Goin' the match?!'

'**OFFICIAL!!!**' roared the pub and left.

Then, they caused havoc on the bus, tube, terraces and telly. But Joe lost an ear, nose and throat on the ferry.

Back at Sally's, Joe burst in bandaged and screamed, '**MUM!!!**, I want me **MUM!!**'

Frantically, Sally pushed him back. 'Hold on, Joe,' she moaned, faking the blob. 'I need a **SLASH!**'

She got one.

## The End

# CUB-COP 2

I was in me basket when I woke up. I yawned and looked about. There was a space in my bowl where my Pal should be. As usual. I got up and shook. Then, I had a sniff at this and that. Then, the doorbell went. So I went out and barked a bit. The Big One came down, clouted me, and let in a bird. I got my nose in quick and got a fucking good snort. He kicked me good and proper for it – but it was worth it!

## The End

# THE HOLY ALE

And lo! Before the Book was The Ale.

In the beginning, Mo woke up in The Wilderness when, suddenly, a celestial bloke landed, saying unto him, 'Mo! Pick up thy slabs and go! For God hath called last orders in Egypt and all thy ale shall turn to blood!'

Quickly, Mo turned his stick into a bus and left.

While he was steering, Mo felt the whole nightmare come flooding back. The Bullrushes, The Parting of the Seas, The Pinnacle of Flame and that fight in The Burning Bush! Just then Mo turned his stick into an Everlasting Pint and stopped.

**PTSSCHH!!!**

Anyway, it is written that a lad came unto the land and with him were some disciples. But they soon vanished when he got nailed up. While he was up there he went, 'Forgive me, father, for I have eaten the Pork Scrolls and now all I ask is a pint!'

So, Sentinel Borgnine passed a gleaming pint aloft.

Suddenly, everything went black...

Two thousand years of Christianity later, a mad Austrian woke up in a museum and went, 'Jesus, I need a pint of empire-quenching dimensions!'

Just then he saw The Ale in a box on a wall.

'Christ!' he roared, in German. 'With a pint like this I could win World War Two!'

He didn't.

# The End

# STINGY'S

Hungrily, I gazed down at my designer dinner and wept. I'd ordered potatoes. I'd got one. A small one. 'Excuse me, waiter,' I croaked, casting a sheepish glance at my clients. 'I don't appear to have an adult's portion.'

'You know ze house rule, m'sieur,' he sniffed arrogantly in French. 'Rich people don't eat. Zey just pay.'

'Ay, lad!' I spluttered, outraged. 'Where I come from this lot wouldn't fill a Subbuteo goalie!'

As one, the whole place turned and stared. At **ME!** I felt the clammy wet mounds of my buttocks grip the seat. A hideous smell enveloped us. Mine. They made me feel small. Very small. My dinner seemed bigger. Unnaturally bigger. 'What's in this soup?!' I screamed, shrinking rapidly.

'What soup, m'sieur?'

By then the place was in an uproar and my potato was massive. Recklessly, I scrambled up onto the table, ran across my plate and jabbed it. 'I can't eat all this,' I squealed, shrilly.

'As I said, m'sieur,' He snorted haughtily in French. 'Rich people don't eat. Zey just pay.'

## The End

# PA!

It was way back when I was a boy and my Daddy was Sheriff of Two Creek Gulch, just west of the prairie. I remember it well. Pa was kicking shit in the saloon when the news hit town: Big Bad Bob Black had busted out and was coming to git my Pa.

'Yup,' went Pa, releasing a young strumpet from his chaps. 'Seems to me a man might get to need a whole shitload of deputies in these parts round about now and I aim to do it.'

Well, Pa ran hisself ragged trying to raise a posse that Sunday morning but all the men were in church being nagged by God and there wasn't a decent gunhand in town.

It was around about noon when the train pulled in and Big Bad Bob Black got off it. With a quick spurt of speed, I raced back to town looking for Pa. He was in the saloon drinking on his own.

'Come on in, son,' he slurred, habitually. 'Seems to me everyone else is in church being nagged by God.'

It was just about then that I was gonna tell him that Big Bad Bob Black was gonna bust in any second when he did!

'Go for your guts, Sheriff,' Bob bellowed, blasting Pa across the saloon.

It would have made a great movie, 'cept for the end, that is.

# The End

# SPOCK OFF!

'Beam up me, Scotty.'
'Aye aye, Cap'n.'
**ZING!**
**WHOOSH!**
'Aaaaaah! Perfect entry, Scotty!'
 Sssss.
'Captain!'
'Bones.'
'Bad news, Jim. Virus in the Officers' Mess.'
'Shit!'
'Exactly. Plus! There's a homosexual in the crew.'
'How do you know, Bones?'
'Spock's dick tastes of shit.'
'Is this true, Spock?'
'Effemitive, Captain.'

## The End

# THE HOR

I woke up wet and flat out in a bog when suddenly an owl hooted and it all came flooding back...

I was driving in the rain, the windscreen wipers were beating: **'FLAP-FLAP! FLAP-FLAP! FLAP-FLAP!'** The trees were rushing quickly past and between them me and my car, lost.

Just then I saw it: a black castle in a lightning flash! I swerved to avoid it and crashed to a halt.

When I woke up my eyes had fisheye lenses on them. She was close, very close. Too close.

'You must help me!' she urged, urgently. 'I'm the only one left of a kids' coach party that crashed here twelve years ago and I've been a prisoner ever since!'

I could feel her looking at me when the door creaked open and a huge retarded servant loomed up at me. '**LUNCH!** is served.'

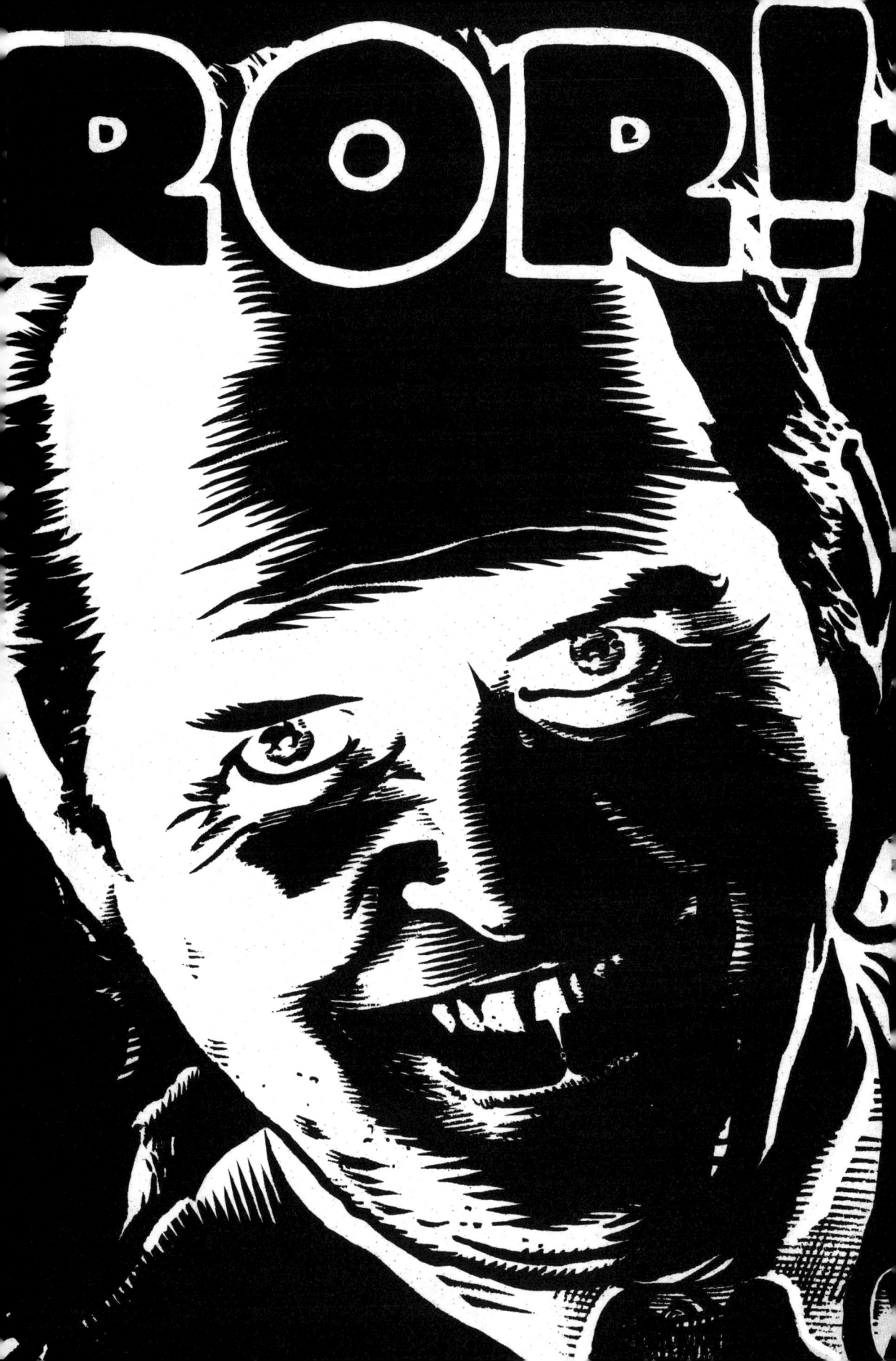

They were round the table when we got there. Their eye followed us as we sat down. Their beak snapped as they hissed in the gloom.

'Good evening, Councillor Wigan,' they went, correctly. 'I hope your room's satisfactory.'

'The only room in here,' I roared, 'Is the one in my stomach where that chicken's going!'

'Help yourself,' they said, indicating the food in the gloom with claws.

So I quickly wolfed and nibbled a bit before ploughing on into a large order of casserole, grill, roast, main dish and, the pierre de resistance, fish. '**GOULASH!!!**' I spluttered, haemorrhaging loudly. 'Hog jowls! No! Perhaps spare ribs first then fat back with sour belly, pork pie, pig knuckles and bacon. **PLUS!** Chitterlings, haslet, cracklings, hard cheese and lard with bread!'

While I was stuffing it in, they told me about the ghostly stomach that played the piano at night in the gloom, the lip that wormed loudly into women's swimwear and the floating scrotum that had suffocated a dozen healthy young schoolgirls in as many years.

'Where's the bog?!' I groaned, holding back six beef curry yoghurts and custard. '**FAST!**'

And that's how I got here.

At least I still had my doggy bag.

# The End

# SOHO!

**WHACK! WHACK!
WHACK! WHACK!
WHACK! WHACK!
WHACK! WHACK!
SQUIRT!**
'That'll be fifty quid please, luv.'
'OOOOF!'

**The End**

# BLOOD

He woke up smelling of blood and lager. All around him men were drinking, women were dancing and dogs were fighting; chairs were flying, windows were smashing and the barman was punching a bloke in the throat. It was Saturday night in Davey Jones's Locker and Hulk Hero was drunk.

Just then, Pat launched forward with a fiver. 'Ay! Hulk Hero!' she spat, thrusting two jugs at him. 'This is your last night ashore so sup up and dance!' Hulk lurched boldly to his knees and vomited. '**HA-HAH!**' he went, loudly. **SPLOSH!** On the dance floor, sailors and their slags were clapping, stamping, yelling and banging their feet on the deck. Hero grabbed Pat and stormed into the heaving mass with a brave yell of glory. '**YOOP!**'

Suddenly, a knife appeared in him and he shuddered to a halt. He span round, fists, teeth and buttocks clenched for combat. Before him stood the giant brutal figures of Ugly Jack Lagerstein and his crew.

'That's my bird Pat you've pulled!' Jack roared, smashing a bottle to his lips.

'I'll drink to that!' Hulk laughed, ripping a lager from his leather, a Holsten from his holster, a Budweiser from his belt and a Foster's from the fridge. **SLOSH!**

Lagerstein steamed with rage. 'Step outside, ship shite, and we'll settle this like men!'

With an unnatural scream of terror, Pat threw herself on Hero. 'Don't go, Hulk!' she begged, slipping a Luger into his Levi's. 'He'll kill you!'

'He'll have to sober me up first!' Hulk belched, casually. 'Pass me me pint, Pat!'

Quickly, with all the ruthless energy of a brewery, Lagerstein surged forth and dashed Hero's pint from his lips. '**AVAST!**' he roared. 'I'll have no man drink in the face of death!'

'Is this The Face of Death?' Hero asked. 'I thought it was Davey Jones's Locker!'

Crazed with rage, Ugly Jack Lagerstein punched Hulk on the head, loudly. Then, he did it again. But Hulk would not go down. The crew gasped at the ferocity of their skipper's attack and stood back.

'**HA-HAH!**' boomed the barman from behind the pump. 'You'll have to do better than that, mate!'

**WASH!** Hulk forced back his forty-third pint and jerked the gun from his jeans. 'Look,' he went. 'Pat's my bird now and I'll kill to keep her!'

'**HA-HAH!**' laughed the barman. 'You'll have to, mate!'

Suddenly, Lagerstein pulled a pistol from his pocket. The lights went out and two guns blazed in the dark. A woman screamed, a man gasped and a body hit the deck. Then the lights went on. All hands were shocked at the sight of Hulk Hero lifelessly spreadeagled in a lagerpool.

'Oh, Jack!' Pat cried. 'He made me do it! It's you I've loved all along!'

Just then, Ugly Jack groaned and collapsed to the floor clutching at a bullet wound with a bloody hand. 'It's too late, Pat. I'm scuppered!' And with that, he sank.

Sensibly, Pat threw herself on Hulk Hero and woke him with a kiss. 'Oh Hulk! Thank God he missed you!' she cried, smothering him with her special ways. 'It's you I've loved all along.'

'Good!' Hulk said, struggling to his knees. 'Make mine a pint!'

## The End

# THE HANGING TREE

'Around now is the time a year when a man wants nuthin' more than to jest up an' hang folks,' drawled Duke, pursing his lips and nodding his head as if remembering what he'd just said before he could go on. 'Yup. Round about now is jest the right time fer a hangin'.'

'Well,' grinned Buck, shooting something. 'There ain't no point in hail us jest sittin' round talkin' about it, Duke. Seems to me we jest owe it to ourselves to jest rush out there an' string one up.'

With that, the two crop farmers got up and, dusting themselves off, climbed into a battered black pickup and drove it. While they were driving they passed a pool hall and stopped.

'Lookee there, Buck. Ain't that one of them damn pool halls?'

'Sure is, Duke. An' I got me three dollars here says I'll whip yo ass.'

'It does?'

'Keerect, Duke. That's just what it says every time I listen to it.'

Buck jumped down from the pickup as the sound of loud fiddling drifted toward them through the open doors of the pool hall. Duke spat a jet of brown juice into the dust and sighed.

'What about the hangin' then, Buck?'

'We got jest about all day fer the hangin', Duke. A man's gotta have some beer an' nicotine fer he can jest up an' hang a man fer nuthin'.'

'Reckon you'd like to bet on that, Buck?'

'You're durn right I would, Duke. Reckon I got me about another three dollars here that says I'm one thousand per cent right.'

Grinning, Duke called over a passing stranger. 'Hay thar, old timer. Does a man need anythin' fer he jest ups and hangs somebody?'

'Well, son,' said the man, puzzled. 'Seems to me like a man would need a whole shitload o' beer an' nicotine fer he could do a proper job. Yup.'

Just then Duke swore and, grabbing a wrench from the dash, hit the stranger several times on the head.

'Sheee-it, Duke,' laughed Buck, clapping his hands. 'You is the sorest loser I ever saw!'

# The End

# Detective Sgt. FORD STOCKWOOD in POLICE BUSINESS!

**SHE** woke me. The light was on. It was white. I could feel her breath.

'Ford… Ford… come on. The inspector's on the phone. He says it's urgent!'

I saw her. She was woman. All woman. Her eyes were black in the glare. She seemed pale. She was trembling. I could feel her.

'Come on!'

I punched her with all I had in the neck. She went down. She was all there in the corner. Eighteen-and-a-half stone of sensual meat. She was there alright. I could taste her.

'Ford!'

I was there. Close. Her breasts filled my hands. Her thick lips open. Slightly. I bit her. Deep. I felt my teeth sink in. I could hear the blood roaring. It was hot. I bit her again. I felt the sharp pain of her fists in my ribs. I wanted her. I wanted her **NOW!**

I sprawled on top of her, ripping her shirt. I spread her. I could taste her blood in my mouth. She was damp. I could feel her teeth in my cheek. Her breath was strong, fast. She was racing. I launched one off to her head. Left uppercut.

'Yes, yes, yes…'

She was animal, all animal. Her mouth was hot and massive. I smashed my lips against it. I pushed her back, biting all the time. My heart was pounding, pumping. It seemed to fill up my throat. I couldn't breathe. She filled me. My fist full on her flesh. She needed it.

She got it!

'You've got forty-eight hours!!!'

'No sweat, Chief!'

She came in then. She looked all busted up. Her face was blood from where I'd punched her. The little purple marks of my teeth stood out on her neck in a circle. Her housecoat fell open and I caught a glimpse of her thigh. I felt the heat.

'Forty-eight hours! You got that Stockwood?! Forty-eight hours!'

'No sweat, Chief.'

I slammed down the phone and was on her. It was cruel. It was brutal. It was violent. But she loved it.

# The End

'**BINGO!!!**' hooted Max, brandishing his coupon wildly at his Mum. His Mum didn't say much. She never had. Not since that accident back in '68. The one with the pool hall. These days she stank a lot. But Max wasn't thinking of the stink, not now he'd won the pools. All he could think of was all the breasts, buttocks and beer he could buy immediately.

Just then, a car pulled up in the drive and an ugly, large-breasted woman sprang out and rang the doorbell. Enthusiastically, Max catapulted to the door and wrenched it off. Instantly, his eyes, tongue and knob popped out. She was the only woman he'd ever seen except Mum. But she didn't move much these days. She just sat there and stank.

'Hello, handsome,' breathed the woman, snaring him in her warm female trap. 'My name's Pat Barlow and I need a room. I've been driving all night through the desert in the rain and I need a bath and something hot and filling inside me.'

'**YOOP!!!**' Max hollered, brandishing his coupon between them. 'I've just won the pools!'

Pat thought quickly. This was her chance. All her life she'd drifted from one bar to the next waiting for this moment. And now her wildest dreams were fulfilled: a pensioner with money! She licked the throbbing wet length of her lips. 'Why don't you slip into something more comfortable,' she purred naughtily, brazenly flattening her front against him. 'Like **ME!**'

'**BINGO!!!**' yelled Max. 'I'll do it! I've always wanted to meet a woman! Especially an ugly, fat woman with huge tits... like you! Why don't you come and meet me Mum?!'

Slowly, Pat edged past him into the damp darkness of the gloomy vestibule and grunted. 'Pooo, honey!' she gasped, wriggling her nose cutely in disgust. 'What's that awful stink?'

'That's just me Mum,' Max grinned, bashing into her. 'Besides, you smell like you could use a barth yourself.'

'Don't pay no attention to that!' Pat roared. 'Just fuck me, here...with **THIS!**'

'**BINGO!!!**' squealed Max, hiding her car in the bog. 'I'll do it!'

## The End

# The WOLF!

The stink of raw meat drifted downwind.
Wild savage snouts snorted at the scent.
Manes bristled in heat.
The pack howled!
The hunt was over!
Wet white fangs all blood they ripped the meat!
Fierce in **BATTLE!** Obedient to **NONE!**
The **WOLF!**

## The End

# 9½ SECS!

I was sitting in the snug of The Mysterious Duck and Rambo brassiere enjoying a plate of bent haddock when a big burly bully burst in. He was six foot seven in his battered leper-skin Levi's and I could tell straight away that he had a cock on him that'd make any woman want to spread out and **SHUNT!!!**

    Instantly, I crossed and re-crossed my legs, rapidly exposing my thighs, suspenders and cap but he only had eyes for his nine-and-a-half pints.
    Nervously, I thundered across the bar and bashed my breasts into him. 'Sorry,' I giggled, naughtily. 'I haven't got the hang of them yet. Why don't you come up this entry, back at my place?'

He downed his ale and, wiping his mouth dry with the back of his huge, tattooed hand, gazed hungrily at the soft curves of my pert, young handbag.

'Lob lunch?' he enquired casually, leveling his gut bazooka at me. I felt my floodgates open and I shivered as a pint of hot stuff gushed out. Then, he roughly tore aside the flimsy damp fabric of my thermals. Panting and straining, I arched back over the bar to accommodate the full throbbing length of his arm. Tipping my cap to a rakish angle, he awkwardly straddled me and plunged in a belly banana of awesome proportions. I gasped as his purple-headed power python punched past the pouting portals of my love entrail, painfully. Then, he drove it in and out relentlessly.

The regulars cheered when he insensitively blasted a bucketful of gut-grease into me. 'Aaaaaah!' he went, and stickily paddled off.

That night, I lay awake in a wet bed and wept.

# The End

# ADMAN

So then we went for lunch at Freebie's. It was packed with freeloading, lager-swilling Filofackers from every ad agency in Covent Garden, as usual.

'Two Squirts and a menu,' I ordered rudely, sliding my feet under the table. 'And make it fast!'

'Can I have the same, please?' my partner at Wheel Robbem Connem and Shaftem, 'Paranoid' Pig Botha, mumbled. 'If that's all right, sorry.'

'Listen, Paranoid,' I went, reluctantly. 'I'm worried. I haven't stolen an idea all morning.'

'Oh, my God!' wept Pig, drastically. 'But the script for the Pork-E account has to be in by tonight!'

Just then, a tall pale bloke with a large nose leapt onto the table. **'HA-HAH! LAGER!'**

Instantly, twenty thousand fivers lit up in my head. This boy had talent and I knew it. Anyone who could drink twelve lagers without looking was talented enough for me! Quickly, I bought him a round. 'My name's Annex Azulu and this is my partner, 'Paranoid' Pig Botha. What's yours?'

'Another twelve pints of lager!' he demanded dynamically in his shoes.

His name was Buff. Beef Buff, a cult author from the north and all his ideas were new. Another twenty thousand fivers flashed in my head. If anyone could write a copyline for Pork-E Snax, it was him.

'Hay, Buff,' I probed, plagiaristically, toying with my Singapore noodle. 'What do you think of Pork-E Snax?'

'Crunchier than a cupboard!' he roared.

Twenty thousand fivers later, I won an award and laughed.

# COP!

Women like uniforms. When I'm in one I feel big and tough. You can rely on a cop. Not like women, children and animals. I hate them. Ever since that day I got hit in the head with a cricket ball I'd wanted to be a cop. Now, all the pubs I go in are empty and I get free beer. I always get the best spec at footy matches, too.

At night we like a laugh in the van. Usually we get pissed up and arrest anything not in uniform. Sometimes we go to strip clubs and fuck about. We do what we like. Last week we caught this kid with a big bag of smack. We all had a bit and threw up in the van. It was cut. So was he.

It's like the Sarge says: 'If they're poor, they're against the law!'

## The End

# CONTENDER

**DING! DING!**

**Round One.**

'...And the crowd roars as the boxers spring out from their corners and circle each other their heads lowered their muscles tight their gloves glistening in the overhead glare from a thousand-watt bulb. Yes! This fight has all the hallmarks of being the bloody carnage and general uproar that boxing is meant to be! Can erstwhile farm labourer, Wolfgang Hod, wrench the crown from the head of triple champion, Bob O'Armstrong? That's the question on everyone's lips tonight.

Oh! And it's a knockout! Well, that was unexpected!'

## The End

# EPIC!

Doctor Lom screamed for silence and got it. 'Members and Genitalmen! Tomorrow begins a great adventure for mankind. In this strange craft here,' he stated, indicating a tug of heroic proportions, 'I shall endeavour to fly, sail and tunnel around the globe until I accidentally discover a lost world full of monsters, mysteries and men. All I need is a plump, young volunteer from the audience to kill things when we get there.'

A deathly hush fell over the tweed-clad members of the Rich Explorers Club as the Doctor cast a hopeful eye around the bar. All had scaled vast mountains, plumbed the depths of mighty oceans, and some had even travelled in time, so it came as no surprise as the first healthy gale of laughter swept over him.

Instantly, a young barman tore through the tweed toward him. 'I'll go!' he blurted, youthfully revealing his jodhpurs.

'Don't do it, kid!' shouted Doug McClure from the bar. 'You'll be typecast forever!'

However, after a lot of burrowing, escaping and fighting, they found themselves trapped by a huge Modelasaurus at the edge of an erupting volcano when, suddenly, from out of nowhere, me mum turned off the telly.

## The End

'Fear not, woman. For it is written that the Lord shall provide!'

'Amen!'

Gunter looked up to see a huge figure in black looming before him. 'Who the hail are you?'

'The name's Ten, sinner, the Reverend Mac Ten and I'm a man of God!'

'Ah, you'll be wantin' a beer then?'

'Yup,' said the Preacher. 'I'm awake, ain't I?'

Gunter called into the shack for beer. They waited. The hot sun baked the pigless earth. They were sweating. Gunter called into the shack for beer. They waited. The hot sun baked the pigless earth. They sweated some more.

'Sure is hot,' said Gunter, after a while.

'So are the flames of Hell, sinner!'

Then Pat came out with the jug. The Preacher took one look and stiffened. 'That's a mighty fine woman you got there, blasphemer. A woman like that makes a man wanna rut hogs!'

'Hogs? Hah!' scorned Gunter, wolfing his beer. 'There's been no hogs in these parts for nigh on twelve year!'

'Avast!' the Reverend Mac Ten hollered as a pig ambled smugly toward them.

'It's a miracle!' Pat gasped, her ripe bursting glories swelling against the Preacher.

'Let's eat,' drooled Gunter, wrestling the pig to the ground.

\* \* \* \* \*

'More pig, Reverend?'

'Nope. I'm gutted,' he said, sliding back his stomach. 'You can't beat the Lord's pork!'

'That sure was one helluva fine pig there, Preacher. Jes' where in the hail did it come from?' drawled Gunter.

'That weren't jes' no ordinary pig there, sinner. That was the career of God, the work of His Hand, the labour of His Love… That was His pig.'

'No shit?!'

'And what's more, Gunter Larson, pig farmer, the reason why no swine doth trot forth upon the land is the wrath of God. For thou art naught but the cock of Satan!'

'The hail I am!'

'Y'all know about the flesh, boy?'

Gunter counted his tooth with the finger of his hand. He counted the wife.

'I'm on a mission from God here, boy. For as sure as God sent Moses and raised him up, he sent me, the Reverend Mac Ten, to Scudsville, Georgia, to save yo ass from hellfire and damnation. So help me God. This is not off the top of my head! I am a fanatic! An enthusiastic crusader! A holy-minded, hot-gospellin' psalm-singin' bigoted puritan here to do God's job! I tell you, pig farmer, and you listen good! I am here to weed out you sons of Belial, you accursed backsliding sensualists. And that's not all! I tell you right now: God is gonna destroy, abolish and annihilate us. Then he's gonna gut, burn and scupper our cities! He's gonna slaughter and kill! He's gonna spoil, rob and ruin! He's gonna ravage, run amok and be violent! Then he's gonna stamp out, sit on, squash and consume us! Man is a Vandal, a rusting tartan worm; an effeminate, slack, limp, groggy infant and God is gonna shit on **US!!!** Cos he's a holy bouncer! A youthful, lusty gymnast, more than a match for us! We're fat, fucked, famished and finished! This ain't off the top of my head! We've got to repent, sinner! Now, you take this woman here! **PAT!** Can't I just see her body blaspheming right here in front of my very eye?! Look at it! Its lustful voluptuousness! Its brothel-haunting shape! Its uncensored bed-hopping heat!'

'No shit!'

'It's God's bidding that I save this woman, for surely she is the Devil's work!'

'Well, if you think it'll do any good, Preacher.'

'Goddam, I know it will! Gunter? Don't you ever wonder why there's no pigs on this here land?'

'Yup.' Gunter counted his ear with the finger on his hand.

'Because you is a dumbass motherfucka and that's why I'm just gonna take this woman here and walk right on out. And you ain't gonna do a damned thing about it!'

'I ain't? The hail I ain't!'

'Make your move, pig farmer.'

Gunter counted his saving with the finger on his hand.

Just then, the Reverend Mac Ten ripped back his cassock to reveal the glossy length of his Peacemaker. He leveled it at Gunter's head. 'Meet God, Gunter!'

Suddenly, the squeal of a thousand pigs erupted smugly toward them. Gunter catapulted onto the porch. As far as his eye could see in every direction was pigs.

'It's a miracle!' gasped Pat, her ripe, bursting glories squirming all over the Preacher's peacemaker.

'You can take her anyhow,' said Gunter, up to his neck in livestock. 'She's alright, I guess, but you can't beat the real thing. Sure as hell there ain't nothing like the smell of hog to make a man wanna git down and **RUT!**'

## Amen.

# BANK-U-THANK!

I woke up. Quickly, I dashed into a Royal Bank of Scotland.

'It... It's my account,' I stammered, timidly. 'I want one!'

'Right!' a big bank bloke in black bags and bomber barked. 'Pull up a peasant and **SQUAT!**'

I did it!

'You give us your **GRANT CHEQUE**,' he begged blatantly. 'And we'll pay **INTEREST** on your **CURRENT ACCOUNT** if you stay in credit.'

'Stay in credit?' I pondered, puzzled as Pooh in a pot. 'What's that?'

'It's when your quid's in the black,' he laughed. 'But when it's not we'll give you a **FREE OVERDRAFT** of up to **TWO HUNDRED AND FIFTY QUID!**'

'**TWO HUNDRED AND FIFTY QUID!!!**' I roared, catapulting.

'Yes. That's **Q.U.I.D.**' he spelt, speculatively.

'**CRIKEY!** That's good enough for **ME!**' I squealed.

'**PLUS!**' he boasted, ripping out **FOUR FAT FIVERS**. 'How about some **FREE DOSH!?!**'

'**OOOF!**' I gasped shamelessly, opening an account. '**YES PLEASE!**'

'Thanks for listening,' beamed the bank bloke. 'Have a nice day.'

'**I WILL!**' I yelled.

**I DID!**

I put my money on a curry.

It was hot. Too hot. For **ME!**

## OFFICIAL!

# BANKER!

Dick Champion was **TOUGH! A SPUD** of a man! He had to be. He was a Royal Bank of Scotland Manager!

'**CASH!!!**' he roared, hugging a packet. '**I LOVE IT!**'

Then, tipping his toupee to a rakish angle, he fingered his button and laughed.

And that's when Pat squeezed in. She was a student. She had a hairdo and several boxing trophies.

'**OOOF!**' gasped Dick, clocking her **GRANT CHEQUE**. '**OI!**' he yelled. '**GIZ IT!**'

'Why…?' she went throbbily, noticing him. He was the first **REAL** Bank Manager she'd ever met.

We'll give you a **FREE OVERDRAFT** of up to **TWO HUNDRED AND FIFTY QUID!'** Dick relaxed unexpectedly. '**PLUS!** Interest on your Current Account!'

'**CRIKEY!**' Pat shuddered, noisily. 'Are all Bank Managers like you?'

Dick bit a quid and ripped out his wallet. 'Fat chance… **PAL!** What other bank would give you… **THESE!**v Snarling, he brandished **FOUR FREE BIG BLUE BEAUTIES**, legally.

'**OOOF!!!**' Pat gasped bashfully. '**FIVERS!**'

Then, eagerly opening her account, catapulted out. Dick wilted behind his desk, a tear in his eye. It was a joyless, thankless, profitless job. But it was worth it.

# OFFICIAL!

# CASH-U-STASH!

It's a good job being a Royal Bank of Scotland Manager, see. Take last week. Slobbering, a student sprang in. Instantly, I smelt a grant cheque. **HIS!!!**

'Why would I bank with you?' he went suspiciously, fingering his Filofax.

'Coz we don't charge interest on pre-arranged overdrafts of up to **200 QUID!**' I screamed horrifically. 'Not to mention our free European travel competition!'

He was impressed! He signed! With a pen. **MINE!**

So, I gave him **FIFTEEN QUID!**

'**YOOP!**' he roared, triumphantly. '**FIVERS!**'

Quickly, I promised him a cheque book, cheque card, Eurocheque card and a Cashline card. **PLUS!** Post card.

Suddenly, he burst into a fit of high-spirited antics.

'And you can use over four thousand **CASH MACHINES!**' I bawled blatantly and, grabbing the lad, charged loudly out into the bank.

'**LOOK!**' I laughed, victoriously. 'We've bagged another!'

Everyone went **MAD!**

Back at my desk I slipped into a fresh tie and got ready to hand over more **CASH!** 'This is a good job,' I mused over muesli.

It was!

# OFFICIAL!

# A FISTFUL OF FIVERS!

'**MONEY!**' laughed the Royal Bank of Scotland Manager.

'**Giz it!**' I roared, my wallet grinning bravely in the sunlight.

'Unnaturally, we don't charge interest on pre-arranged overdrafts of up to two hundred quid!'

'**YOINKS!**' I blurted, my knitwear tightening.

'And you can use over 4000 cash machines throughout the land,' he bragged, sliding a wad toward me. 'Open an account and I'll give you these three free fivers. Then you can scoop your loot wherever you want!'

Quickly, I slid him a quid. My quid.

He promised me a cheque book and a cheque card.

**PLUS!** A Cashline card.

'Now, sign here,' he grinned.

**I DID!**

**OFFICIAL!**

# THE PROFIT!

'THIS IS THE DEAL!' quoth the Royal Bank of Scotland Manager.

'Giz it!' roared the mob.

'Listen!' he said, his wallet bulging heroically in his pocket. 'There shall be no interest on a pre-arranged overdraft of up to **TWO HUNDRED POUNDS!** Free banking! **PLUS!** Many thousands of **CASH MACHINES!** And unto those students who open an account will rain **THREE FREE FIVERS! EACH!!!** And they shall say unto themselves, **'OOOF!!!'**'

And Lo! With an almighty roar, the ground opened and swallowed the lot!

So...

Only one student was left, and she won all 125 prizes in the European travel competition. Thus! She woke up in a European city!

'Huh?!' she went, unnaturally. 'You wouldn't get this happening at any other Bank!'

## OFFICIAL!

# THE HUSTLER!

'Hay, Pa?'

'Yes, son.'

'What in the tarnation's a **GRANT CHEQUE?**'

'Why, that's what them Royal Bank of Scotland folks'll do just about anythin' fer.'

'Really Pa?! Really?! Would they chew the saloon spittoon with a spoon, Pa?! Would they?!'

'Yep. I reckon they would, son. And that's me sayin' it, too.'

Gunter smashed the pack and beamed. It was the first shot he'd played all day and he sure wanted to beat his son, Piglet, badly. He hadn't slept two nights for thinking about it.

'We sure could do with a **GRANT CHEQUE**, son,' Gunter went on. 'Why, that there bank is so crazy, they'll give **TWENTY POUNDS FREE** to anyone who's got one.'

'Gosh, Pa! That there's more money than... than...' Piglet didn't know what it was more than. He just knew it was more money than he'd ever seen before.

'See, son, that gosh-danged real fancy Royal Bank of Scotland has more money than sense. Why, they'll give you a **FREE OVERDRAFT OF TWO HUNDRED AND FIFTY POUNDS!** An' **INTEREST** on Current Accounts. Too!'

'Wow, Pa! Will I ever have one of them plum clever **GRANT CHEQUES**, Pa? Will I, Pa?'

'Nope. They don't take pigs at school, son. But you can sure shoot pool better'n any hog I ever saw. And that's me sayin' sum'p'n! Even if I did say so myself. Didn't I?'

'You sure did, Pa. You sure did!'

# OFFICIAL!

# SWEET SIXTEEN!

I was born. Then got bored and went to sleep.

Sixteen years later I woke up. The alarm hadn't gone off. Still, it wasn't all bad. I'd missed maths!

Suddenly, I landed a job and needed a place to stash my cash. **FAST!**

'Why should I open an account with you?!' I snarled at the Royal Bank of Scotland Bank Manager.

'Lady! We've got **CASH MACHINES!**' he screamed horrifically. 'And plenty of 'em!'

'**YOINKS!**' I gasped. 'Can't you do better than that?!'

He was breathing. We both were. With our lungs. I saw his eyes. With mine. Somewhere, a bus passed, a dog barked, a disco opened.

'**HA-HAH!**' he barked back. '**NO PROBLEM!** We'll give you fifteen quid!'

'That's a **LOT!**' I shot.

'Yup!' he went, economically.

Quickly, I opened the account and scooped the loot.

'Try your luck with our free competition,' he added, enthusiastically.

'**I'LL DO IT!**' I did. **I WON!**

Next! I wake up in a European City! A big one! It was full of foreigners.

**GOOD!!!**

# The End

# APPENDIX!

Aidan Hughes & Malcolm Bennett. Photo by Ilkay Mehmet. 1986

# THE BIRTH OF *BRUTE!*

There was no star in the East. No kings gave gold, frankincense or fucks. No donkeys were inconvenienced. No squatters occupied a manger.

What did happen though was that the giant form of a young Malcolm Bennett interrupted the light in the doorway of the Riverside in New Brighton, Merseyside, casting a menacing silhouette into the ballroom. There, Aidan Hughes sat chugging lager with his crew, eyes everywhere. He noticed Malcolm. Everyone did. And though they'd not met before, he knew who he was. Everyone did.

And everyone knew Bennett was not only radical but dangerous, a reputation he kept to his dying day but one that did not put Hughes off meeting him. Quite the opposite. Not even after he approached Hughes' table and loudly demanded he be sold drugs before a massive fight invited a police raid and brought their first meeting to a premature end.

Drugs would unite them again, like love, when they met at a dealer's place of business and discovered they lived next door but one from each other. Not that this knowledge oiled the wheels of neighbourliness. Bennett continued his policy of never answering his door. Hughes even sent his girlfriend round in nothing but a fur coat and 'Happy Birthday' daubed on her naked body. Bennett slammed the door in her face.

Inevitably though, their paths would cross. They were both well-read, spiky dandies swimming against the tide of mainstream thought and expression. They began to recognise they could work together, fire each other up and make something that excited them. Fuck everybody else.

Soon they would establish a creative partnership so stark, so blunt, so vivid that they had to name it *BRUTE!* The concussive words of Bennett and the explosive illustrations of Hughes formed a marriage made, if not in Heaven, then in Wallasey.

Bennett had attracted attention with his abrasive performance poetry, navigating by the light of Jack London, Erskine Caldwell and Dashiell Hammett toward a minimalist style of writing filled with pubs, guns, guts and the unexpected.

Hughes had been trained as an artist by his father and, influenced by the greats of comic art like Jack Kirby and Steve Ditko and legends of the woodcut Lynd Ward and Frans Masereel, he was able to complement Bennett's words with a kindred directness and force.

They collaborated on the 1981 book, *Battle Poet*, and 1983's *The Claim of Malcom Bennett*, while *BRUTE!* was just a twinkle at the bottom of a glass. The combination of their talents created more than the sum of their parts, something we hadn't seen before. A challenge. Like your eyes were being asked if they wanted to step outside and settle it like men.

But in order to bring *BRUTE!* into the world, our heroes moved from the Wirral to Bristol. And while it wasn't a difficult birth they took on board plenty of medication, just in case.

Battle Poet by Malcolm Bennett. Art by Aidan Hughes. é publications 1981

The Claim Of Malcolm Bennett by Malcolm Bennett. Art by Aidan Hughes. é publications. 1983

Bennett began trying to distill the English language into what he called *'Woodspeak'*, a linguistic device for nailing street poetry to a page recalling tabloid headlines and noir fiction. Together they began publishing the first **BRUTE!** stories in the classified section of the Bristol Evening Post. While it suited the *'Woodspeak'* style, it was too costly for two lads on the breadline to serialise their classified pulp concept at their own expense.

But then a stroke of good fortune propelled the project forward and placed their work in front of an eager audience. Hundreds of copies of *The Claim...* had been ruined by rain damage at the printers. They were offered another print run, or, the printing of another publication, up to 32 pages.

They were ready. They had tons of stories and, anyway, the smaller publication would be easier to lug around than Malcolm's long and heavy polemical poem on his dole application.

And so, in 1984, they produced the first **BRUTE!** magazine, a glorious 32-page A6 glossy bastard. It was an immediate success, selling out its limited run and creating an instant demand for more. They almost certainly had a pint to celebrate. Not only did it thrill the comic book world, it excited the literary critics and the cool kids of the music industry too. Praise was lavished on **BRUTE!** from as unlikely bedfellows as Stan Lee, Oliver Stone, Keith Waterhouse, Neil Jordan, Pat McCabe and George Michael, even.

Even though Hughes had a spell in Amsterdam and Bennett at Her Majesty's Pleasure, the bulk of their stories would be developed while they struggled to get by in Bristol. They managed to produce six more editions of *BRUTE!* over the next four years along with the paperback *BRUTE! Classified Pulp Nasties*, all featuring their trademark snarling artwork and punchy prose, garnering a broad audience that included Kazuo Ishiguro, Vivian Stanshall and The Pet Shop Boys and glowing praise in the Literary Review, Time Out, The Face, Creative Review and the NME, among many others. They had arrived, and on their own terms, with an uncompromising slab of ferocious illustrated literature.

Despite selling every copy of the *BRUTE!* paperback, Sphere Books refused to do another print run because the Catholic League of Decency had picketed a bookshop in Ireland after becoming offended at the depiction of God as a chain-smoking speed dealer. Thanks to His Divine Mysteries, we are unable to confirm or deny the accuracy of this portrait.

*BRUTE!* was originally intended to be an experimental novel written in 'Woodspeak' but, as they continued to develop their distinctive style, it evolved into full-time black comedy by the time they moved to London and *BRUTE! #3* came out in 1985.

By *BRUTE! #4* every image had developed an iconic quality. And every line was a slap in the face, at least.

Malcolm had become a semi-regular on TV thanks to his charisma, good looks and massive gob. Hughes was producing artworks and storyboards for Warner Bros. and the BBC. *BRUTE!* naturally lent itself to TV too, the pair producing a film short, *Love Me Gangster*, the animated series *Brute's Adventures Of Sizzler* for Channel 4 and *Mallet!*, the film short about the eponymous psychotic DSS Fraud Investigator,

23: — lurching forward, hooks it into the HOOD's nostrils.

A BAD MOVE!

24: The HOOD squashes ROCKY head.

OOOF!

27. The BABE stands holding a smoking gun.

28/ From a C/U of the HOOD, who lies dead on the wharf, the CAMERA spins back to reveal TWO COPS holding ROCKY.

WHEN THE BABE PLUGGED HIM. I TOOK THE RAP FOR HER. DUMB, H

 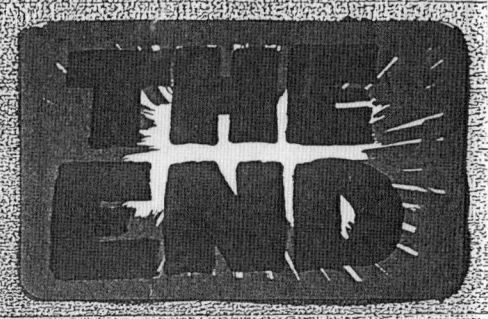

29. ROCKY laughs insanely ~~from the~~ in the ELECTRIC CHAIR.

/0 ROCKY: "BUT THAT'S ME ALL OVER………

SUCKER!

©copyright Bennett & Hughes October 1988.

Storyboard sketches for 'Rocky!' by Malcolm Bennett & Aidan Hughes. MTV 1985

Aidan Hughes & Malcolm Bennett. Photo by Richard Watt. 1987

made for LWT. Written by Bennett, with graphics and art direction by Hughes, they featured many of their key themes: menace, crime, cleavage, guns, violence, revenge and lust. Cor!

Barely believable but true stories showed how life and art had begun to blur. Having missed out on a magazine's booze cruise, Bennett and Hughes risked life and limb by jumping off a bridge onto the boat like thirsty action heroes. Then there was the time that Malcolm fired a crossbow at some retreating hoolies or when he strode naked into a drug dealer's with a MAC-10 machine pistol, for a laugh, like.

By **BRUTE! #7** they were trying to fit **BRUTE!** in with working full-time in advertising and TV. Proof, if it is required, that full-time work is evil and wrong. By this time Hughes had got married and moved to West London, Bennett's girlfriend had walked out of their South London home and the '80s media gravy train had hit the buffers. Then there was Bennett's increasing drug use and its consequences. He was fired from one TV show for showing up high and armed and another for firing a gun live on air, burning a fat girl's arm with the dispensed casing. Suddenly, no one would hire him. And because of their association, no one would hire Hughes either. So getting together to work on black comedy became less attractive despite their highly successful alliance. At this stage, they were black comedy.

It's hard to look at their TV work and not be reminded of Frank Miller's *Sin City*, the 2005 crime anthology movie based on Miller's graphic novels, currently awaiting a TV reboot. Some would say there would be no *Sin City* without **BRUTE!** Whether that's true or not, it certainly represents a classic style that warrants revisiting, echoing as it does a golden age of illustration whilst smashing your senses in the face with something entirely original and darkly comic.

Hughes' startling illustrations spawned a number of exhibitions in London, the USA & Czech Republic. But the page is their natural home and what you have in your hand is a rare combination of like-minded sparky lads who, for a few brief years, produced something special together that looks just as brilliant and urgent today as it did in the Eighties (whenever that was).

As the writer & film critic, Anne Billson once wrote of **BRUTE!**, *'In future, all novels will be written like this'*. OK, that didn't happen, but that only makes this collection all the more exceptional. This is what you could've won.

Malcolm Bennett & Aidan Hughes. Photo by the unknown. 1986

# MORE!

BRUTE! No. 1 by Malcolm Bennett & Aidan Hughes. é publications February 1984

BRUTE! No. 2 by Malcolm Bennett & Aidan Hughes. é publications March 1984

BRUTE! No. 3 by Malcolm Bennett & Aidan Hughes. é publications September 1985

BRUTE! No. 4 by Malcolm Bennett & Aidan Hughes. é publications April 1986

BRUTE! No. 5 by Malcolm Bennett & Aidan Hughes. é publications December 1987

BRUTE! No. 6 by Malcolm Bennett & Aidan Hughes. é publications / Titan Books December 1988

BRUTE! No. 7 by Malcolm Bennett & Aidan Hughes. é publications / Titan Books May 1989

**BRUTE!** Colossal, work-hardened men! Wild untameable women! Savage, unbridled passion! Raw and erotic tales of gut-wrenching drama and suspense!!

**BRUTE!** Romance, cruelty and religion! Sport, crime and agriculture! Horror, western and football!!

**BRUTE!** The cult comic of the 80s now unleashed in paperback! Tough and dynamic! Packed with hilarious non-stop laffs!!

'Unmatched in contemporary British comic art' CITY LIMITS

'Tough and dirty' THE FACE

'Graphic, gruesome and hilarious' BLITZ

'In future all novels will be written like this' TIME OUT

'Masterly' LITERARY REVIEW

0 7221 1565 2   CULT/GENERAL FICTION

UNITED KINGDOM £1.95

ISBN 0-7221-1565-2

BRUTE! Classified Pulp Nasties by Malcolm Bennett & Aidan Hughes. Sphere Books 1987

BRUTE! Forbidden Planet book signing flyer. 1987
Right. BRUTE! 'Get Your Farting Gear Round This!' & 'Mine's A Pint!' T-Shirts flyer. 1987

# THIS IS WHAT THEY SAY!

*In a selfless bid to research stories for future generations, these plucky proletarian poets have hurled themselves into a life of danger and immersed themselves in the murky world of crime, guns & drugs. It was a sacrifice that was to bring great rewards – this book! The best experimental novel this decade.*
– **KAZUO ISHIGURO, BOOKER PRIZE & NOBEL PRIZE WINNER**

***BRUTE!** is to modern English what graffiti on New York subway trains is to Modern Art. Masterly.*
– **KEITH WATERHOUSE, LITERARY REVIEW**

*A pocket riot bible of screaming bold text and b&w prints that sets itself apart from everything else. I loved it!*
– **JAMES BROWN, LOADED MAGAZINE**

*The pulp friction of **BRUTE!** makes all the characters of Spillane, Sin City and Tarantino films look like Nancy Boys!*
– **MORT TODD, EDITOR OF CRACKED! & COMICFIX**

*The thrusting, penetrative re-entry of **BRUTE!** is proof enough that you don't have to go to fucking art school to create some good honest red hot splatter.*
– **KEVIN ALLEN, DIRECTOR & PRODUCER**

*In future, all novels will be written like this.*
– **ANNE BILLSON, TIME OUT MAGAZINE**

*Tough & dirty. The literary equivalent of a flying brick.*
– **THE FACE MAGAZINE**

***BRUTE!** is Malcolm Bennett and Aidan Hughes' baby. It's a bad baby. It spits and it swears.*
– **NEW MUSICAL EXPRESS**

*This is woodspeak. A blunt sawn-off, pump-action dialect designed for the very purpose.*
– **BLITZ MAGAZINE**

*The women are brutal. The men are brutal. The dogs are brutal.*
– **MELODY MAKER**

*It's as hard as a bull's prick in a freezer. It's as sweaty as Sly Stallone's buttock fluff – but twice as sexy. **BRUTE!** is brill.*
– **NEW MUSICAL EXPRESS**

*Liverpool's answer to Sam Peckinpah! Eat your heart out, Pulitzer!*
– **TIME OUT MAGAZINE**

**OFFICIAL!**

# Sheath-Bursting Romance

## Keith Waterhouse

**Brute!**
(Ed) Malcolm Bennett & Aidan Hughes
é Publications 32 pp Unpriced

THE MOST economical short story opening I know is one of O Henry's: 'So I went to a doctor.' We are past the first act even as the curtain rises.

If Mr Lawford Gates, in his contribution to this new collection, does not reach that masterly standard, he strives some way towards it with the first sentence of 'Pub Action!':

> Just then a bloke erupted into the snug with a fiver.

We are pitched at once into the middle of the story. Wasting no time in establishing character or atmosphere, the narrator plunges ahead with his response to the bloke's entry, which is to kick him in the head, butt him in the stonks and tear off his ears. Unfortunately, Mr Gates then slackens his pace somewhat, allowing his hero a meandering change of scene where he pukes in a pram full of smack and is pumped full of slugs. There is little development. The narrative ends much as it began:

> I leaned over and, punching my arm up him, grabbed his tongue and quickly pulled him inside-out. The sleeve of my Tacchini suit top was fucked. But it was worth it! The End.

Padded out to nearly 350 words, 'Pub Action!' is over-long and repetitive. It would have been a useful exercise for Mr Gates to have pared it down to just over 50, the length of Mr I Barker's 'Cub-Cop!'. It is illuminating, or anyway possible, to quote 'Cub-Cop!' in full:

> It's a good laugh being a police dog, see. Take last week. Slobbering, I burst in this room, the lads in blue behind me. I barked. Instantly, these three punks left this big bag of coke and bolted. I leapt in and got a fucking good snort before the cops kicked me off. But it was worth it! The End.

Note how the two stories echo one another's ending. Both authors being new to me, I do not know whether Mr Gates has influenced Mr Barker or the other way round. Both, I would guess, have assimilated much of the minimalist anonymous writing to be found on the walls of such inner-city urinals as survive in an age of education cuts.

JULY 1986

*Brute!*, subtitled 'Sheath Bursting Romance!!!' is the fourth such collection of 'classified pulp nasties' as they are called. Its nine stories can be read in less than ten minutes – or more realistically, among the readership it is aimed at, in less than ten hours. It boasts a sale of 5,000 copies per quarter – a respectable figure for any little magazine (of which *Brute!* must be the littlest, measuring only four inches by six and containing a mere 21 pages of text). Most of its readers are – strange choice of verb by its publisher – 'admitted' to be 'probably young', and for them it is claimed that 'they are the people who are more aware of what "modern English" is than anyone else'.

It depends what you mean by modern English. *Brute!* is to modern English what the graffiti on New York subway trains is to modern art. It is the expressionism of the inexpressive, the literature of the sub-literate. Alarm at the decline in reading standards can only subside from a study of these tales. If the young are to regard a story such as – say – Mr Jock Hudson's 'Bloke-U-Poke!' as 'modern English' ('Rock Buttock was a slut. One day, when he was in Greaseby Bum Baths, a bloke saw his bum. He said 'That's a fine looking shit hole you've got there, Rock . . .') then perhaps they would be better off watching video nasties (most of these tales could be the book of the film).

Alternative humour – ie, farts are funny – is there. Point and purpose are absent. The surrealism is that of the abstract painter who never learned art throwing a pot of paint in the face of a public who never learned art appreciation. What we have here, as in so much modern work, is ineptitude passing itself off as anarchy – the blind conning the blind. The significance of *Brute!* is that this is what we have come to.

Critique of BRUTE! by Keith Waterhouse. Literary Review July 1986

# OFFICIAL! LETTERS

**A SOLICITOR WRITES**
Dear Mr Waugh,
I regret to inform you that my clients, Mr Malcolm Bennett and Mr Aidan Hughes of BRUTE! magazine, were deeply offended by Mr Keith Waterhouse's article about their publication in your July issue.

They feel that he has maligned the good name of their innocent readers, to say nothing of calling them blind! Messrs Bennett and Hughes would like to know just what it is that Mr Waterhouse has against blind people. PLUS! He had the audacity to compare the work of New York's subway/urinal scribblers with the work of their team of writers, some of whom fought in two wars for their country!

However, referring my clients to your own article in the July issue I have been able to restrain then from taking any legal or Pub-Action. Still, they do demand the right to reply to such a grave defamation of character. I would appreciate it if you co-operate, after all, it's the least one can do for two such plucky war veterans.

Thank you.
**Hans, Christian and Ersön, Solicitors**
London SW6

---

**BRUTE REPLIES**
Dear Keith,
Our mum went mad with us when she read your bit about us in the *Sun*, or whatever it was, last month. She even hid our bus pass so we couldn't go down the pub. She cried for days.

Anyway, Keith, as you can see, you've caused quite a rumpus in the BRUTE! camp these last few weeks, and by now you should have heard from our solicitors, Messrs Hans, Christian, and Ersön. We'd also like to add a few points as to where you went wrong in your article.

See, Keith, in modern entertainment the vast majority cry out for the instant image; tabloids, pop videos, advertising, *etc*. Yet you wouldn't believe just how much stuff our authors send us, and what crap it all is! Old men, it seems, have got nothing better to do than to churn out this long stuff. Writers are so self-indulgent, always blabbing on about their problems and that, (much like yourself, Keith). What we do next is to apply the BRUTE! writers guide (enclosed) to their material.

Besides we were editing magazines before you were old enough for your feet to touch the shithouse floor, never mind write on it! Keith, you've got to admit that

things have got to change in literature, it has to be brought up to date, and if the young won't take up the banner, as they have in music, film, etc., then it's up to us old folk to show them the way. We just haven't got the time anymore to read whole books, and especially books about women having bayonets shoved up them like that sick TWAT Thomas writes about. It's not even funny!!! PLUS!!! Now that adventuring and exploring seem dead we are left with endless tales of neurosis and degeneracy. No, we haven't got the time for that stuff. Besides, our mum won't let us have thick books in the house. In this manner we hope to win people from the cathode-ray tube back to literature. Our books are FAST, FUNNY, ORIGINAL, and, what's more, READ!!! Which, we think, proves a point, huh, Keith?

Yours literally,
**Malcolm Bennett**
(Retired)
**Aidan Hughes**
(Never worked)

PS We demand a bar in every library!!! Why don't you write about that in your articles in the *Sun* instead of going on about throwing stones at clay pits in Sheffield. A bar in every library will bring your average punter roaring back to books!!!

---

> BE A *BRUTE!* WRITER
> AND MAKE A QUID!!!
>
> ★ ★ ★
>
> The English language is littered with useless words. The concept of BRUTE! is, by abolishing these words, to tell a story in the simplest manner possible.
>
> Words actions, deeds and descriptions, *etc*, are minimized. Entire plots are done away with.
>
> BRUTE! is extreme.
>
> BRUTE! is graphic.
>
> Miller, Kafka, Hesse, Kerouac, Sartre, who are all crap, are equally guilty, with their vain, psychiatric overwriting, of conspiring to hold back the revolutionary process of word construction. Slang, dialect, and mispronunciation, are all integral to the evolution of the language.
>
> Basically, writers that have no pain in their sex and no sex in their pain, are not really writers at all. They are fish.
>
> Good luck!

SEPTEMBER 1986

BRUTE! response by Malcolm Bennett & Aidan Hughes. Literary Review September 1986

BRUTE! Forbidden Planet book signing. Photo by Dick Jude 1987

Right. High praise for BRUTE! from chief Bonzo Dog Doo-Dah Vivian Stanshall. October 1986

>                                    The Still,Standing House
>                                    71 Hertford Road
>                                    London N2 9BX
>                                    30 October 1986
>
> Monsters the both of You,
>                        having just consumed my first Brute
> (No.4 'Sheath Bursting Romance!!!) courtesy of a purported chum -
> I cannot rest until I own your entire catalogue.
>   No newsagent I've tried will admit to having knowledge of you or
> your publications. And I have twice been slapped in the describing
> of it. May I buy from you direct? Please send your list whathaveyou.
>                        Your plain englishness has
>                        knocked the shit out of me
>                        leaving only a gaping want!
>                        And no mistake.
>                                    *Vivian Stanshall*
>                                    Vivian STanshall

# OFFICIAL!

# AUTHOR!

# AIDAN HUGHES!

When Aidan and Malcolm went their separate ways, Aidan continued to work successfully as a commercial illustrator, as he does to this day. His dramatic high contrast artwork would translate easily to advertising and animation, even if clients like Guinness and Bank of Scotland required fewer murderous, bloke-poking, pub heroes.

Aidan also produced several large scale outdoor murals in England, France, Italy and the Czech Republic. But perhaps Aidan is best known for the album covers he designed for Massive Attack and the German industrial band KMFDM, featuring the unmistakable style that runs through his body of work. He currently lives, works and has a great time in the Czech Republic.

Aidan Hughes. Photo by Zuzana Hughes. 2019

Malcolm Bennett by Aidan Hughes. 2015

# MALCOLM BENNETT!

Sadly, Malcolm passed away in March, 2015, of unknown but unsurprising causes. While his post-*BRUTE!* years were punctuated by pubs, drugs and prison, by the turn of the century he had cleaned up and started a new life in London. He told few about his previous life on TV, radio and page, yet he couldn't shed the contrarian charisma that would establish him as a racontrepreneur in his stomping ground of The Borough.

Malcolm began writing and performing again, enjoying a revival around 2010, when the discovery of previously unpublished *BRUTE!* stories led to the release of *I, Brute!* in 2010. He published small runs of new material in the following years and was looking forward to the future when he went and fucking died. He is still painfully missed.